KW-222-254

TOWN BRONZE

Julia Murray

Chivers Press
Bath, England

•

Thorndike Press
Waterville, Maine USA

This Large Print edition is published by Chivers Press, England, and by Thorndike Press, USA.

Published in 2003 in the U.K. by arrangement with Robert Hale Ltd.

Published in 2003 in the U.S. by arrangement with Robert Hale Ltd.

U.K. Hardcover   ISBN 0–7540–8901–0 (Chivers Large Print)
U.K. Softcover   ISBN 0–7540–8902–9 (Camden Large Print)
U.S. Softcover   ISBN 0–7862–5106–9 (General Series Edition)

The text of this Large Print edition is unabridged.
Other aspects of the book may vary from the original edition.

Set in 16 pt. New Times Roman.

Printed in Great Britain on acid-free paper.

British Library Cataloguing in Publication Data available

CHAPTER ONE

Doubtless it was the young woman's shabbiness that had made the coachman treat her so. But she had no more than two pennies left in her reticule at this point in her journey and surely to have parted with them just now would have been foolhardy indeed. She had always intended to present him with some largesse, but being obliged to pay sixpence for a mug of scalding coffee and a fat sandwich at the last stage had reduced her slender hoard considerably. But her cloak-bag, battered and patched already, now lay in the muddy puddle where he had tossed it and the fellow had whipped up his team without so much as a glance in her direction. Eliza sighed philosophically and gingerly retrieved her belongings from their watery resting-place. She had no doubt that she would find her only presentable gown sadly stained and wondered if it would be possible to rescue it from yet further ill-treatment.

A two-mile walk now lay ahead of her. She had half-hoped that Sophy might have sent Tom with the gig, but it was no surprise that the lane before and behind was equally deserted. With a sigh she pushed her hat more firmly onto her brown curls and glancing ruefully at her now leaky boots set out briskly.

1

She had progressed barely ten yards, however, before she heard the unmistakable sound of a carriage approaching. Even before it came into view she could tell it was travelling at a considerable pace and, suspecting it to be driven by one of those dashing young blades who have no thought for anyone but themselves, she made a desperate attempt to climb up the bank at the side of the road. But the bank, like the road, was wet and muddy. Her boots lost their hold, she fell onto her knees and her cloak-bag tumbled back into the roadway. To her intense mortification the ancient lock gave way, the bag burst open and her meagre belongings cascaded directly into the path of the approaching vehicle.

There was an exclamation of annoyance, audible even above the snorting of startled and highly-bred chestnut stallions. The driver of the curricle had pulled sharply upon the reins, dragging the beasts to a shambling, rearing halt, and issued a staccato command to his diminutive groom. Springing down from his perch at the rear, this gnome-like individual, with some peril to his life, succeeded in grabbing the bridles of the panicking animals. The gentleman, a man whose driving-coat alone declared his lofty social standing, swung himself into the road and turned a somewhat fiery gaze upon the cause of the trouble.

Realizing her brown pelisse was ruined anyway, Eliza sat down in the muddy grass and, her cheeks burning with mortification, raised her eyes to his face. Although in his late thirties he was well enough looking, she could see that at a glance, with raven hair and a strong, aquiline cast of features, including a most powerful and determined jaw. Assuring himself that his valuable pair had suffered no lasting damage, he turned to her again and said in a voice of ice: 'I trust, madam, that you are now satisfied with what you have done? That my animals have not been utterly ruined is immaterial. Indeed,' he added, glancing at Eliza's scattered petticoats, 'had I realized the nature of the obstacle I should have had no hesitation in driving over it.'

All vestige of shame vanished with this speech. Sliding down into the road, Eliza answered haughtily: 'Indeed, sir, I am very much surprised that you did not!'

He was looking at her now and his first impression, that she was some local girl searching for firewood whose baby had unaccountably tumbled into his path, was swiftly revised. For Eliza, at twenty-four, was by no means beyond that bloom which had, a few years earlier, proclaimed her a more than usually pretty girl. Mortification had brought a flush to her cheeks and the anger she felt at the stranger's manner had lent a decidedly militant sparkle to her normally calm grey eye.

'In fact,' she continued, raising her chin challengingly, 'I should appreciate it very

3

much if you would remove your vehicle and let me gather up my belongings in peace!'

Further revisions were taking place beneath those carefully ordered black locks. The person before him was unquestionably a gentlewoman and, if her present attire was shabby and her underwear, as he had already noted, plentifully darned, it merely signified that she had fallen upon evil times. Something of a twinkle entered his dark eye, therefore, and he regarded her with a little less disfavour.

'Would it be a great impertinence, madam,' he began silkily, 'if I were to ask what you intended to do with your belongings? It would appear that your valise is somewhat beyond repair.'

The truth of this robbed Eliza of an answer. Glancing to where her dresses and petticoats yet lay, she saw that not only was the lock broken, but the ancient bag had finally succumbed to ill-treatment and split along one seam. She knew he was laughing at her, however, so with a tolerably superior air she told him that it was no concern of his and she would be grateful if he would merely remove himself from her presence.

By this time the gentleman's interest was fairly caught. Not unintelligent, he had already realized that it was his own precipitate approach that had caused her downfall and, since he was, at this moment, feeling magnanimous, he decided it behoved him to

4

come to her assistance.

'Where are you bound?' he asked, somewhat abruptly.

Eliza raised her chin. It was, after all, a futile question, since the lane led to one place only, Malham village, and the one or two mansions that lay in its vicinity. So she answered tersely: 'Malham, sir.'

He raised his brows. 'The village?'

She nodded. She had no intention whatsoever of revealing her precise destination.

'Then you had better let me take you. It is a two-mile walk, at the very least, and you cannot, surely, bundle your belongings under your arm like some washerwoman.'

'Thank you, sir,' she responded in her haughtiest manner, 'but the prospect does not dismay me and, besides, you were travelling towards Bath, not the village.'

He smiled suddenly and Eliza was privileged to see that which had caused the downfall of many a maiden since he had come upon the town seventeen years before. Indignant as she was she felt herself responding and was instantly horror-struck that at her advanced years she could still succumb to the charm of a handsome smile. But the moment's hesitation had been enough. The gentleman issued a command to his groom; by a series of deft manoeuvres the vehicle was turned and the now perfectly calm

5

animals stood ready to take her to her destination. It only remained for Eliza to gather her muddied possessions as best she might in the remains of her cloak-bag, bundle the thing under one arm and accept the gentleman's assistance into the awkwardly high vehicle. In a moment they were moving, the gentleman setting his beasts at a gentle trot and Eliza, trying hard to forget the mud on her pelisse and the strand of hair that hung across her cheek, sitting very still and straight beside her escort.

She was relieved that he did not try to make conversation. That he might attempt to discover something about her had been part of her dread; for what could she say that would not simply compound his no doubt inferior opinion of her? Consequently, when they shortly rolled past the small square of grass that composed the village green, she thanked him civilly and requested that he might set her down. Briefly the gentleman seemed reluctant and she wondered if he would insist on knowing where she was going, but then he smiled and in a moment she was standing at the side of the road, her bundle, like washing, under one arm, and the gentleman was turning his curricle and driving away.

Eliza sighed and permitted herself to wonder for the first time who he was. Some notable Corinthian, she had no doubt, probably visiting one of the families that chose to live just outside Bath, the FitzLevens, perhaps, or the Palmers. But really it was no concern of hers and, turning her back on the vanishing curricle, she set out for Malham Park.

The gentleman's rapid assimilation of Eliza's circumstances had been more accurate than he could have known. Miss Woodeforde was indeed a gentlewoman; in fact she could claim relations with several honourables, a general who had fought Napoleon, and had an uncle who was an Earl. But her father had been a nobody. Having, at a young age, fallen in love with quite the wrong young lady, he had been disinherited, sent to India and forgotten. His marriage to an impecunious young woman of good family some years later had not softened his father's heart and when this gentleman died shortly afterwards there had been no mention of Clarence in the will. But the new Earl had been made of softer stuff. Clarence had returned to England with two daughters, Agnes and baby Eliza, and since Mrs Woodeforde had just died it was generally thought that Something should be Done. Agnes had been given a home and proceeded to grow up in all the comfort and luxury of an ancient home. On Eliza Fate had not smiled so kindly, although in later years she was to consider herself more fortunate than her wealthy, pampered sister. She and her father had lived a ramshackle existence, travelling restlessly about the country, while, one by one, all Clarence's schemes had failed. When Eliza was thirteen, and Clarence's health dwindling, he had finally taken a post as Italian master in a select seminary for young ladies and had managed, by smuggling his daughter into as many classes as possible, to give her a more than passable education. When he died, as penniless as ever, Eliza had been equipped to find a Position and this she had done, with a nip-farthing old gentleman who preferred not to send his daughter to one of the country's more select, and expensive, seminaries. The girl was fourteen, a mere six years younger than Eliza herself, and a gentle tender-hearted creature. The fact that she found Italian difficult and arithmetic impossible was but a temporary set-back, for Sophia Crawley proved herself a dear and Eliza loved her. Sir Lucius Crawley was somewhat different. To be sure, he swore he doted on his daughter and at times this almost seemed to be true, but not when it came to putting his hand in his pocket when something needed paying for.

At eighteen Sophia no longer really needed a governess and Eliza had started to talk of seeking another post. But as far as Sir Lucius was concerned, he had no intention of parting with her; he would not have admitted it, but he could not have run the house without her and indeed had not known such comfort since his wife had died, many years before. So Eliza remained and was not sorry, although her salary was meagre and her room poky and she was not allowed to light a fire in it until the middle of December.

Her recent journey had been to wait upon her sister Agnes. This female was now Lady Marchmont and had summoned her sister to aid her as her time drew near. Eliza had obliged, although reluctantly, for Sophia had become an uncommonly beautiful girl and had begun to attend the Bath assemblies under the aegis of Lady Winterton, whose own daughter, Jennifer, was about the same age. Eliza's greatest fear was that Sophia, who, besides being beautiful, was heiress to quite a sizeable fortune, would fall prey to one of the London bucks who generally retired to Bath when 'the dibs were out of tune' and it behoved them to keep out of the way of their creditors. And this indeed appeared to have happened, just as Eliza had feared. A scribbled note in Sophia's childish hand had led her to abandon her sister to the tender care of the midwives when the baby was barely delivered and hurry home to see just what on earth Sir Lucius had been about. Sophia's note had been largely unintelligible. She had seemed indeed quite happy about her forthcoming engagement, but Eliza could not be sanguine and the additional information that Cousin Susan had arrived had sent a chill through to her soul. This female, an unmarried daughter of Sir Lucius's eldest sister and now in her forties, had been trying for many years to gain an entrée to Malham, generally on the pretext of Taking Charge of Sophia. Since she was obliged to provide for herself out of what anyone else would have considered a handsome income, she was perpetually on the look-out for some largesse and admittance to Malham Park had been her ambition for years. The fact that she had achieved it at last seemed to Eliza to indicate that Sir Lucius had finally taken leave of his senses, since he had in the past been used to speak of her in far from conciliatory terms and had shouted at her from the attic windows whenever she had tried to visit.

These same windows could now be seen by Miss Woodeforde as she neared the top of a small rise in the rutted drive and in a moment the house lay before her, a modern edifice, built during the reign of George the first. Compared to the Marchmont Eliza had just left it was a cottage, but to Eliza's eyes its lines were pleasing and elegant, not so large that one might lose oneself within a maze of passages, nor so small that the inhabitants lived one on top of another. The sight of the house served as a considerable spur to the young woman. She could clearly distinguish the light from candles in what she knew to be the dining-room and realized that it was in fact considerably later than she had thought. Indeed it was nearly dark and if she did not hurry she would almost certainly be late for dinner.

She was not, but she had been considerably relieved that no one but Keen, the butler, had impeded her progress as she entered the house. She requested that he might inform Sir Lucius of her return and, ignoring Keen's stunned expression, hurried upstairs, quite forgetful of the dishevelment she had displayed. When she entered the drawing-room the party had already assembled and it was clear from the start that she had interrupted something. News of her return had plainly been conveyed, for Miss March, her greying curls arranged with unbecoming severity about her gaunt features, sniffed audibly and Sir Lucius merely grunted, adjuring the late-comer to look lively, as they had waited an hour already. Eliza did as she was bid, pulling the bell-rope to summon Keen and only then turning to observe her charge.

Sophia was wearing a new dress and it became her. Her corn-coloured hair was best displayed by stronger colours and to Eliza's surprise she was wearing a gown of mid-blue crêpe, matching almost exactly the colour of her eyes. Since Sir Lucius had resented every penny spent on finery she could only attribute that persuasion, and good taste, to Cousin Susan and reflected that here, at least, she had done some good. Sophy had approached her unobtrusively and now kissed her cheek.

'How glad I am you are come!' she exclaimed in a low voice. 'You have no notion of the hobble I am in, but I made sure you would fix it.'

There was no time for more. The servant announced dinner and Miss March had risen somewhat regally. To Eliza's surprise and amusement Sir Lucius held out his arm to his niece with old-world courtesy and they proceeded into the dining-room, where the lady took her place at the foot of the table as though it had always been hers. Despite Eliza's return—and she had always regarded the young woman as an interloper—she was in high spirits, but Eliza could not find much to enjoy in her choice of conversation. Sophia's letter had contained the name of her betrothed, but the writing had been so appalling that it could not be deciphered and it was only now that she began to realize that Sophia had made A Catch. Miss March's conversation turned almost entirely on what Sophia should expect at Ingham Place, no doubt the seat of whatever gentleman Sophia had bewitched. But since the most of it was calculated to tell Sir Lucius just how imperfect Eliza would be at educating his daughter for her new position Eliza felt herself well able to hold her tongue and let the others play their part.

'Of course,' Cousin Susan was saying, with a false smile at Sophy, 'you will find it *much* larger than Malham! Oh indeed! Why, when I stayed there with Mama on one occasion I recall being quite amazed at the miles of corridor and at the number of servants it seemed necessary to retain!' She smiled at Sir Lucius. 'Of course,' she continued, 'Miss Woodeforde will be quite unfamiliar with such a household, but, I assure you, it is quite within my ken! You are fortunate, Sophia, that I am here to instruct you.'

Sophia hung her head and said nothing.

'To be sure,' the lady continued cheerfully, helping herself to a second pigeon, 'it is bound to be quite awesome for you at first, poor child! But when we have done something about your manners I'm sure you will feel much more the thing.'

Sophia looked up quickly, a deep flush rapidly colouring her cheeks, and Sir Lucius, who had maintained hitherto an uncharacteristic silence, said caustically: 'If there is aught amiss with my Sophy's manners it is because she has not the brazen ways of the London beauties. And in my opinion she does very well as she is, so let her be!'

Miss March tittered. 'Oh Lucius, my dear, how droll you are! Naturally I did not mean— only she does lack a little Town bronze, even you must admit that, and while Miss Woodeforde is doubtless very well in her way—'

'I will have you know,' Sir Lucius interrupted again, 'that Miss Woodeforde has an Earl for an uncle, a half-dozen honourables as cousins and the Lord knows how many of old Nosey's generals as relations! As far as I am concerned Miss Woodeforde's education of my daughter has been precisely what it ought, which is doubtless why this Foxcroft fellow thinks so dashed well of her.'

'*Foxcroft*?' exclaimed Eliza, staring. '*Julius* Foxcroft?'

'Aye, aye, that's the fellow! Capital, ain't it? Rich as a Nabob, and he chooses my little Sophy!' He chuckled as he spoke and, reaching over, patted his daughter's hand with some affection.

Eliza was silent. She had never met him, but she had heard so much about the gentleman that she had no desire ever to do so. Not only was he twice her Sophy's age, he was a confirmed rake, with a string of mistresses and indiscretions to prove it. And thus was Miss Crawley's urgency explained. Overwhelmed by the nature of the proposal she had doubtless been unable to refuse and now, with both her father and her cousin so exultant, she had found herself trapped. She wondered what such a loose fish as Foxcroft had found to amuse him in Miss Crawley. To be sure, she had a reasonable fortune, but compared to Foxcroft's own it was negligible and, besides,

14

she possessed none of the arts or skills of the accredited London beauties that must have been so much more to his taste. But after some frowning consideration Eliza changed her mind. It could be that this was the very thing that had captivated him, that artless appeal that Sophia had in abundance. And if he truly loved her—but here Eliza shook her head decisively. From what she had heard of the man he was incapable of any human, moral feeling. She became aware suddenly of a silence about her and, glancing up from her fierce contemplation, she saw that everyone was looking at her.

'What the devil are you shaking your head for, young woman?' Sir Lucius demanded tersely. 'That champagne was the finest I'd had in a decade and what's more you weren't even there!'

Realizing the conversation to have drifted far from the original topic she reddened and muttered that her thoughts had been on other topics.

Sir Lucius was about to express a sarcastic desire that Miss Woodeforde might attend to the conversation when he caught his niece's eye and, guessing this very reproof to be in her mind also, said gruffly: 'Well, well, I dare say it was not worth attending to in any event.'

Very soon after dinner, pleading tiredness, Eliza retired to her own room. She sensed her presence to be resented heartily by one

15

member of the company at least and, as for Sophy, well, she knew the girl would come to her room later. She came sooner than Eliza had expected. A gentle knock heralded her entrance and, barely glancing at Eliza, she plumped herself upon the hard little bed and sighed.

'If only Cousin Susan would not pester me so!' the girl complained, twisting one long curl between her fingers. 'If only she could realize how much I wish to forget Ingham and Mr Foxcroft.'

Eliza eyed her gravely, but continued to remove the pins from her hair. 'You do not like him, I collect.'

Despairing blue eyes met concerned grey ones. 'Oh Lizzy, it is so . . . ridiculous, like a fairy tale! Why should he bother with me at all? I'm sure I did nothing to encourage him, although Susan says I must have done to make him ask for my hand.'

'Have you met him a great many times?'

Sophia frowned in thought. 'Well, the first time was in the Pump Room, when one could hardly not notice him, you understand, for he was so very fine, not at all like the gentlemen one usually sees, like Peter Warkwith or Mr Handsby! He asked Lady Winterton to perform the introduction and although I think she did not quite like it she did so. But he said so very little to me, how could I guess he had formed a . . . tendre for me?'

Eliza shook her head. It was quite baffling, to be sure. 'When did you meet him next?'

'At an Assembly, in the Upper Rooms. Really, it was most odd. I'd told him I was to attend, you see, when I met him first of all, and when he came he stood up with me for two country dances and then left! Wasn't that odd? Jennifer was quite wild with me, for she seemed to think he had come only to see me, but I can't believe—but it did seem quite particular, Lady Winterton remarked upon it.'

'As well she might!' Eliza murmured thoughtfully. She could hardly believe that such an experienced Bond Street Beau could make the mistake of singling out one country girl, and wondered how many other damsels had been as mad as fire over it. 'And after that?'

'I didn't see him again, Lizzy, at all, until he came to call upon Papa! And when Papa told me what he had said, that he wanted to marry me, well, I couldn't think what to do! So I wrote to you.'

'I see.' Eliza thought rapidly. 'Is the engagement official?'

'I don't think so. At least, I have no ring, but Papa talked about an announcement, or some such thing, in the *Gazette*.'

Miss Woodeforde's heart sank. It seemed as though Sir Lucius had wasted no time whatsoever in ensuring that this very valuable fish did not slip through the net. 'I suppose,'

17

she said slowly, 'that you do not wish to marry the gentleman?'

Sophia stared up miserably. 'I don't know him! He seems a stranger and he's so old! And when Susan talks of Ingham in that odious way and how I shall have to behave I feel I would rather die!'

This dramatic announcement, even accompanied as it was by a muffled sob, made Eliza smile. 'Don't worry, darling, I shall not let you marry the old gentleman.'

'You won't? But what can you do?'

'Your Aunt Jemima, darling, are you not her legatee?'

Sophia nodded. 'Yes, but she lives in Bedfordshire, somewhere, and is considered quite an eccentric. She hasn't seen me since I was a baby.'

'Would she help you, do you suppose?'

The girl shook her head dismally. 'Papa makes me write to her once a year, so she will not cut me from her will, but she never answers and has probably even forgotten who I am.'

'Never mind,' Eliza responded with resolution. 'Your Aunt Jemima will serve us very well.' She thought for a moment. 'Where is Mr Foxcroft now?'

'He left this afternoon, for London, I believe, but he has rooms at the York House, in Bath, and Papa said he should be back within a week.'

'A week? That is excellent! Dearest, don't worry. When Mr Foxcroft returns he will find a most formidable dame awaiting him and if what she has to say does not make him change his mind then nothing ever will!'

CHAPTER TWO

'But Mama,' Mary persisted, 'however will you convince him?'

'Don't shout, girl!' cried her mama, pressing a hand to her brow and wincing. 'Do you not know that I have the headache?'

'Yes, Mama, I should think the whole household knows!'

'How dare you, Mary! Apologise at once!'

'Yes, Mama. I'm sorry, Mama.'

'You might at least say it as though you mean it,' her mother complained, lying back upon the sofa and shutting her eyes. 'You know perfectly well it is all for you; you might at least show a little consideration.'

'Yes, Mama. Should you like your smelling-salts?'

The Dowager Lady Ludlow groaned. Stretching out a hand she received the glass bottle without gratitude, saying irritably: 'Find your sister, Mary. Make sure at least that that female has her in a clean dress! It is the least she can do, to look presentable.'

'Yes, Mama.' Mary left the room, dragging her feet a little and sighing.

As the door clicked shut Lady Ludlow relaxed. She felt herself to be sorely tried, for not only did she have a husband who had managed to die but he had left her a jointure which, while enabling her to maintain her own establishment in Town and keep herself clothed in a manner that cast many a less well-endowed female into a fit of the blue devils, was nevertheless described by herself as a pittance. Her daughters too were a sad trial. Mary, at seventeen, had yet to overcome her tendency to freckles, while Jane, at twelve, showed herself so disinclined to become a Lady of Quality that she was generally to be found in one of the dirtier places of the house, especially the coal-hole. It had been the one solace of her life that her young brother, although indeed a trial in himself, had so far forsworn the married state. As long as Julius was unwed she could view with a certain tolerance his more extravagant ventures, turning an—almost—deaf ear to the tales of her tattling friends, consoled by the fact that all his wealth would one day be, if not hers, then certainly Mary's. She knew too that it was probable that only Julius's wealth would be able to establish the girl at all creditably. She could not delude herself. While priding herself on her selfless devotion to her offspring she yet had to admit that Mary's freckles, to say nothing of the lingering puppy-fat, would need a deal of getting over. But Julius had money to burn. She had said it often enough in the past, bemoaning the fact that it had all gone to him, forgetting the sizeable settlement her dear Papa had made upon her at her marriage. It only seemed fair that it should come to her family after his death, if of course there was anything left with all the philandering her brother did.

The announcement in the *Gazette* of his engagement had come as a shock. She had delivered a severe rebuke to her eldest daughter when this damsel had screamed out loud, following her casual perusal of the society columns. The headache she had previously had was nothing to that she developed on reading the paragraph dumbly pointed out to her and Mary's wondering remarks had done nothing to assist. When once more in command of herself she had demanded her new writing-desk and had at once penned a letter to her brother in Bath. To be sure, he had not told her he was going there and if her friend Mrs Gilmour had not thoughtfully informed her of his departure she would not have known where to look. Now, however, she did not debate; her summons was brief and peremptory: she had every expectation of seeing her brother in London within the week.

The fact that he did arrive had nothing to

do with his sister's letter. Indeed he left Bath within a day of its being posted. Consequently, though she tried, Lady Ludlow could not be gratified when Mary, on her return from the school-room, announced in piercing tones that a carriage had stopped below.

'If it is morning visitors I am too ill to see them! You had better tell Sexton I am indisposed.'

'No, I think—It's Uncle Julius!'

Lady Ludlow groaned. Mary's shriek had threatened to bring on her palpitations, which thought was barely soothed by the knowledge of her brother's arrival. Mary had rushed from the room. Her affection for her uncle amazed Lady Ludlow, who, moaning and grasping her smelling-salts, lay back upon the sofa in a position of artistic collapse. She could hear her brother mounting the stairs now, or rather her daughter, chattering, as she was, at the top of her voice. She heard her brother's laugh and grimaced. She hoped he was not going to be in one of his frivolous moods. It would all be too much for her to bear. The door opened. Having given him a moment to appreciate the scene she had set she opened her eyes and gave him a look of pained reproach.

'Julius, is it you?'

She held out one limp hand to him, but he ignored it, walking straight to the bell-pull and tugging it violently. 'You know very well it is. I trust I find you well. You look in excellent health.'

His sister was immediately irritated. 'As a matter of fact, Julius, I am far from well and it certainly does not help to have you behaving in my house as if you were master!'

Julius smiled sardonically and, turning, gave his sister her first real view of him. He was very tall and finely proportioned, his chest and shoulders displaying the inclinations he felt for pastimes such as fencing, and boxing at Jackson's Parlour, in Bond Street. Black-haired, he was not handsome, for his features were harsh, but he was possessed of a devastating smile, one that, when he wished, lit his dark eyes with a wickedly attractive twinkle. The smile he gave his sister now was not kind, but she did not appear to notice.

'I declare, Julius, I never met a more unnatural brother! However could you do this to me?'

Mr Foxcroft did not answer, for at that moment Sexton appeared, and he ordered himself some Malaga, and sherry for his sister.

Lady Ludlow sniffed. 'You might at least ask, Julius!'

Mr Foxcroft raised his brows and then, as Sexton left the room, disposed his length in one of his sister's elegant green brocade armchairs. 'Well, Antonia? What is it that has put you so at outs with me?'

'It's the announcement, Uncle Julius, in the *Gazette*!'

Her uncle's eyes twinkled wickedly at Mary, making her giggle, but her mother, perceiving this, was incensed, saying sharply: 'That will do, Mary! Be good enough to hold your tongue or you will go to your room.'

'Yes, Mama.'

'So you saw the announcement, did you, Antonia? Well, in that case I might as well take my leave.'

'If you do, Julius, I shall never speak to you again!'

Mr Foxcroft smiled quizzically. 'I take it, Antonia, that that is a threat?'

Lady Ludlow pursed her lips. 'Julius, you are being deliberately provoking! I requested that you should visit me, in case you had forgot!'

'Requested? When?'

'By letter, Julius! You must have had it!'

'No, Mama, for I only posted it two days ago!'

'Thank you, Mary, I remember quite well!' She breathed deeply for a moment and then said in failing accents: 'Julius, the engagement!'

'Ah, I understand! You wanted to wish me well! That is most kind of you, Antonia, although why you must needs summon me I know not.'

'How can you be so provoking? You will bring on one of my attacks!'

'Uncle, I think you had better refrain.'

24

Mr Foxcroft repressed a smile. His niece, with whom he possessed quite a rapport, was seated across the room and although she clearly enjoyed his sallies it seemed likely she would bear the brunt of his sister's resentment later, so he said gravely: 'Very well, Antonia, my engagement. What did you wish to say?'

'I was never more provoked in my life! Mrs Gilmour actually had the impudence to ask me if I knew of it! Of course I said I did, but when she started asking me about the girl I could tell her nothing! How could you, Julius?'

'How could I what?' he inquired infuriatingly. 'Become engaged, or not tell you?'

'Both! You always knew I wanted Ingham for Mary! I declare it is very selfish in you to do this to me!'

'I don't think so,' Mary said from across the room. 'Why shouldn't Uncle Julius get married if he wants to? I think it's very romantic!'

'It is not romantic, Mary,' Lady Ludlow declared crossly. 'In fact I think it the most ridiculous thing I ever heard.'

Mr Foxcroft's lip curled. 'Indeed! I am not in my dotage, you know. Why should I not get married?'

Lady Ludlow eyed him fulminatingly. 'You are thirty-eight, Julius! I dare say anyone would have expected you to marry before this if you intended to. It is quite thoughtless of you.'

25

Mr Foxcroft rose. 'If you wish merely to rail at me, Antonia, I shall take my leave. I am in no temper for such flummery.'

'Now, Julius, don't take a pet, I beg of you! It is enough to bring on my palpitations!'

'What gammon!' her brother told her cruelly. 'I dare say you are as hale as I!'

Lady Ludlow's bosom swelled, but the door opened at that moment revealing the butler with a silver tray. 'Anyway, here is your wine. At least sit down for a moment.'

Mr Foxcroft obliged, but his expression was grim and he did not speak again until the butler had left. 'Well, Antonia, what do you wish of me?'

'Nothing. Why should I? I believe you malign me, Julius, thinking I care for nothing but myself. Who is this girl, in any case? I'm sure I have never heard of her.'

'There is no reason why you should,' her brother responded dryly, 'since she has lived all her life in a Somerset manor.'

'Has she fortune?'

'I believe so, but in any case it does not signify.'

'Then why, Julius? Who is Miss Sophia Crawley that she so captivates you?'

'Perhaps she is beautiful, Mama!' Mary suggested, jumping up. 'Is she, Uncle? Should I like her?'

Mr Foxcroft smiled. 'She is quite pretty, I suppose, and as for liking her, why, I am sure you will, since you are much of an age.'

Lady Ludlow gasped. 'A school-room chit, in fact! Julius, are you run mad? A girl with neither face nor fortune, and I dare say no class or breeding either.'

'She has both class and breeding,' Mr Foxcroft answered coldly. 'She is also pretty and, I seem to recall, the heiress to a sizeable Bedfordshire fortune. Are you now satisfied?'

'NO!' declared his sister, her bosom heaving. 'You are doing this purposefully to spite me! Look at Mary! How can you do this dreadful thing to my poor darling?'

But Mary grinned in answer to Mr Foxcroft's inquiring look, so he drained his glass and rose.

'I will do my duty by Mary, you may be certain, even though one might suppose it to be rather the task of the present Lord Ludlow, your illustrious brother-in-law.'

The dowager did not answer. Having waited vainly for a moment or two, he set down his glass and said cordially: 'Good-day to you, Antonia. See me out, minx!'

Mary at once sprang up and grasped his arm, but Lady Ludlow, having given her brother one last dagger glance, lay back upon her sofa with her salts.

Besides his sister, Mr Foxcroft had a further call to make before returning to Bath. Sir Lucius Crawley had dispatched the announcement rather too soon for his liking and he had not been surprised to find Lady Ludlow had cut up stiff. But in Brook Street, in an elegant house he had purchased, lived his mother and he could only hope now that she had somehow missed the notice that had so inflamed Lady Ludlow. He was conducted to the drawing-room by the aging butler, but his mother was not there and he was forced to wait some minutes before she appeared, leaning on her maid's arm. Mr Foxcroft frowned momentarily. His mother, a beautiful woman in her day, seemed aged, but then she smiled and he relaxed. Striding forward he took her arm from the maid and guided her to the chair with the straight back he had had especially made.

'Julius, dearest! What an unexpected delight! I understood you to be in Bath!'

'So I was, Mama. Are you comfortable, or shall Millie fetch a cushion?'

'No, darling, I am quite easy. Millie, put the bell on the table where I can reach it, yes, and then you may go.'

The maid bobbed and slid out and Mrs Foxcroft turned with a smile to her son. 'How was Bath?'

Mr Foxcroft grimaced. 'Slow, as you might have guessed! No wonder you did not want to live there!'

'Full of dowagers and gouty old men?' Mrs Foxcroft supplied, laughing. 'You might have guessed it, dearest, when you went there!'

'So I did, but I had a particular end in view.'

'Did you, darling? What was that?'

Her son hesitated. His mother was smiling particularly sweetly at him. He rose and paced the room, swinging round at last to say: 'I decided, some months ago, that it was time I made a change. I've withheld nothing from you, Mama, you know what I am! But if the name of Foxcroft is not to die out I must needs marry.' He grinned ruefully. 'Antonia would say I had no such duty, her own Mary and Jane being quite sufficient, but I cannot think that Papa would agree!'

'Perhaps not, darling, but that is not reason for you to rush headlong into wedlock.'

'I know, and I have not.' He paused and then, seating himself beside her again, said: 'I gather you have seen the announcement.'

The old woman smiled. 'I saw something, certainly, but I decided to pay no attention until you told me yourself.'

'No. Unfortunately Crawley was a little premature. I had wanted to tell you first, but it seems, in his delight, he could not wait.'

Mrs Foxcroft's smile was wry now. 'Her father is very pleased? I cannot own to any surprise, darling! You must be quite a catch for any woman to make!'

'Which is why I went to Bath.'

Mrs Foxcroft's delicate brows rose very slightly.

'However was I to find a disinterested bride

in London, Mama? I'm weary of society maids with their puffed-up consequence and mincing ways! There is not one I should care to share a house with, let alone my life!'

'And Miss Crawley? You can spend your life with her?'

He nodded. 'I think so. She has character but it is gentle and to a large extent unformed. She has no arts or scheming ways. She's an innocent, Mama.'

'And also very young, it seems.'

'Eighteen,' he agreed. 'It seemed better to me. She is more likely to be content with the life I can give her than if she had any very fixed notions of her own.'

'Darling, I do hope you won't catch cold over this.'

He frowned. 'Mama? Why should I? The girl's mind is unformed, but she has been most carefully reared. I'm sure she will make Ingham an excellent mistress in time.'

'But you don't love her, Julius?'

'Is that so important? In my opinion it is grossly overrated. I'm sure we will both come to feel a worthy affection.'

A worthy affection. Mrs Foxcroft's heart sank. She foresaw misery ahead, but she said nothing.

'Witness Father and yourself. You cannot deny that you and he were happy, can you? And yet you married at your father's express wish!'

30

This was true, but Mrs Foxcroft did not mention the years of anguish she had suffered with a husband who did not care for her until it was almost too late and who had forced her to lead a life quite foreign to her experience and inclinations. 'Darling, do you think it quite fair to take a young girl from the school-room and expect her to manage a large house like Ingham without trouble?'

'She will learn and I hope I am not so hard as to expect miracles!'

'No, darling, but you clearly expect her to have little more than an initial difficulty.'

'Mama!' Mr Foxcroft exclaimed, laughing. 'How can you say such things? You have not even met her!'

'No, Julius, but I feel I have a fair idea from what you have told me.' She smiled at her son's perplexed face. 'Tell me, am I to meet her?'

'But of course! I have invited her with her father to Ingham. I hope you will be there to hostess for me. If you do not I must needs ask Antonia and although I'm sure she will be overjoyed at the opportunity to set my little Sophia in her place I feel I simply cannot do it.'

Mrs Foxcroft was silent. She was not one of those possessive mothers she had so despised as a young woman, for indeed she had several times fallen almost into a despair over her son's wild inclinations, wishing he might only settle down, but his description of 'his little Sophia' was quite daunting and she wondered how long it would be before he found himself quite utterly bored. Many were the caps that had once been set at her son. Not handsome, he yet had charm aplenty when he wished, but, while he was quite likely to spout the most flowery compliments to the prettiest of females, he could just as easily deliver a damning set-down, causing the unfortunate lady in question to retire in a hurry. She had thought the time must come when he met his match, but she had always envisaged a girl of spirit and fire, certainly not a carefully protected girl just emerged from the school-room.

'Darling,' she said suddenly, 'no date is fixed, is it?'

Mr Foxcroft shook his head. 'No, for I wanted Ingham to be perfect for her. I am having your apartments redecorated and also the blue drawing-room. But it all takes time and, when I am not there to superintend, goodness knows what these workmen get up to!'

His mother smiled perfunctorily. She was wishing, more than ever before, that she could get herself about without such a fuss. 'When are you going to Ingham, Julius?'

'I don't know. Next week or the week after. Shall I fetch you?'

'No, no, don't do that. I think I shall make

my own arrangements.'

Mr Foxcroft nodded, but there was something in his Mama's frown that made him believe she was planning something.

Before returning to Bath there was another call Mr Foxcroft considered it behoved him to make. While he felt he owed the lady no explanation of his conduct he had never really considered not going and now, as he set out on foot for South Street, he realized he had always regarded the visit as necessary if he were truly to undertake a new life.

The tall house was shrouded in darkness but for a small chink of light gleaming from between the curtains at a first-floor window. Mr Foxcroft did not need to knock, for indeed he had a latch-key, but after a moment's hesitation he pocketed the key again and raised the heavy brass knocker. There was no immediate response, but after waiting nearly a minute on the step he saw a flicker in the fanlight and in a moment the door was opened.

The sombre individual who now greeted him had a face as expressionless as a chunk of wood. He bowed the gentleman in and in a moment had conducted him to the elegant first floor drawing-room.

Lavinia Monks was reclining on a blue-satined sofa. She was an elegant creature, with glistening black hair and a full, red mouth. Her plentiful charms had pleased Mr Foxcroft for some little time, causing him to purchase the house in South Street by way of thanking her. Their association was generally known, although the lady certainly never admitted it, moving as she did in the lower regions of society but with aspirations for higher things. She was a widow, with little money of her own. Destitute, she had used her opulent personal charms to drag herself away from penury and had, at one point, felt almost certain of final success. She had admitted her ambitions to no one, but everyone knew how hard she had tried to bring old Foxey to sticking point.

Turning her head, she contemplated her visitor with shadowed eyes. She did not get up, but allowed Mr Foxcroft to kiss her hand. The butler brought him a glass of brandy without being asked and the gentleman disposed himself as well as he could in one of Mrs Monks's awkward little chairs. The lady herself received a glass of Madeira wine and finally said in her deep, husky voice: 'I did not expect you, Julius.'

He contemplated her in silence. She was a beautiful creature, with the opulent charms that suited his taste. She could not, he thought, have been more different from the girl he was to marry. 'You've seen the announcement,' he said. Everyone else had.

She nodded, her eyes on his face. 'Have you come to say goodbye?'

He swallowed deeply from the glass and

34

said: 'I owe it to my wife to do so.'

'But will you?'

'I will.'

She laughed at him. 'Not for long, I'll warrant! Who is she, Julius? Some little fortune-hunter?'

'On the contrary. I believe she has money of her own.'

'You don't know?' Mrs Monks's tone was incredulous. 'I should have thought that even you, Julius, would have found that out first of all!'

'It did not seem to matter excessively. Miss Crawley herself seemed quite unmoved by any mention of my finances.' He did not say that Sophia had appeared terrified by the prospect of so much money.

'Really, Julius? She had taken you in then!' She smiled at him, but her bitterness showed clearly in her eyes.

'I do not think so,' he answered her shortly, his tone and expression flat.

'Well,' Mrs Monks continued, stirring restlessly against the blue satin, 'she must have had something to tempt you from your comfortable existence. Was it beauty? Is she quite charming? Should I like her, do you suppose?'

'Possibly, though I doubt it.'

Mrs Monks laughed. 'Would she be very shocked, I wonder, to discover how you have chosen to spend your time?'

'Perhaps, but it cannot signify in the slightest, since I have every intention of being a pattern husband.'

Mrs Monks laughed out, the music that had once so charmed him leaving him quite unmoved. 'I wonder,' she said musingly, 'just how many marriages have started along such promising lines. The door will always be open to you, Julius, unless of course you desire that I should leave here?' This thought had not previously occurred to her and as she contemplated Mr Foxcroft from beneath her lashes a cold dread gripped her of what he might say.

But he shook his head. 'No, you may keep it. But you will understand, Lavinia, if I am no longer able to make those other little— contributions.'

Her heart sank. The engagement had been a shock, but she had been foolish enough to suppose that, even though he was married, he would continue to make use of the house as he had always done. The knowledge now that the means of support she had so come to rely upon was to be totally withdrawn filled her with a hollow fear. Rising, she determined on one last attempt.

Mr Foxcroft looked down at her as she knelt beside his chair. Her expression was one of invitation and he felt the old response awaken in him. He repressed it, although he took her face in his hands and kissed it.

36

'Julius, must it be so different? We dealt extremely, you and I. Don't spoil it for some little chit you hardly know! You don't care about her; you couldn't. Ask yourself whether you could ever have with her the fun we have had.'

Her anxiety showed plainly now, although she was smiling, but Mr Foxcroft appeared totally unmoved. 'Yes, we've had fun, I will admit. I dare say no one else could give me just what you have, but you have overlooked one thing.' He rose and gathered up his discarded hat and gloves. 'I went to Bath, my darling, with the intention of seeking myself a bride. You see,' here he looked down at her with a cruel mockery in his eyes, 'it was pleasant enough, I admit, but it had begun to pall. I no longer care for that life, or for any of its trappings.'

Lavinia Monks was drooped against the chair. For a moment she reminded him irresistibly of a drowning woman, but the impression passed and he left the room.

CHAPTER THREE

Mr Foxcroft left for Bath on the following day. He made no further visits except to his tailor, where he chose himself two new waistcoats and selected a coat to be made up from the new superfine just that morning delivered. He drove himself down, in his curricle, with his diminutive groom sour-faced and silent beside him. Being no mean whip, he made excellent time and drew up the steaming, sweating horses before the York House at five o'clock, without having partaken of so much as a mug of ale. His arrival produced ostlers for his horses and bowing footmen for himself. Having ordered refreshment in the way of some cold meats and brandy, he was informed by the lackey that a lady had called against his arrival and was waiting for him at that very moment in one of the hotel's comfortable lounges.

Miss Eliza Woodeforde sat nervously in one of the comfortable chairs and twisted Sophia's kid gloves nervously between her fingers. When tentative inquiries the day before had produced certain information about Mr Foxcroft's return she had known severe misgivings, for it was one thing planning in the quiet of one's own chamber and quite another to put such a daring scheme into effect. But nothing was gained without trying and consequently she had put her heart into the matter and set out for Bath. Being obliged to wait some two hours for Mr Foxcroft's return had done nothing for her courage, but when he finally strode into the room she had recollected her Sophy's plight and had risen to the challenge.

Mr Foxcroft surveyed her coolly. He had no idea who she was, or what she could possibly want, but she was eyeing him with a positively chilling expression in her steely eye. He took in her appearance in a single glance and his eyebrows rose. The sacrifice of an entire night's rest had been worth the trouble. Wearing the deceased Lady Crawley's sables, with her hair pulled ruthlessly from her face and a pair of spectacles poised awkwardly on her nose, Eliza looked complete. She was, Mr Foxcroft decided, wealthy and eccentric and he had no suspicion that they had met before, under totally different circumstances. Recollecting himself, he bowed and was startled to receive in return a look that encompassed him from his glowing locks to the shine that gleamed upon his hessians and which seemed, moreover, to consider him in no very friendly light. His surprise gave way to amusement and he said, at his most charming: 'You wished to see me? I don't believe I have had the honour.'

Eliza was flooded with relief. The horror she had felt when first he entered the room had been sufficient almost to deprive her of her senses and to discover now that either her disguise was perfect, or that he had quite forgotten their previous encounter, made her momentarily forgetful of her present mission. For it was indeed the gentleman with the curricle and his smile had haunted her ever since. With an effort she collected herself and raised her chin with some hauteur. 'Mr Foxcroft? I am Jemima Stanley.'

She held out her hand, which he received, a look of amused expectation on his face. 'Miss Stanley? How may I be of service?'

She sat down and fixed him with a stony glare. 'Miss Crawley is my niece,' she told him awfully.

'Is she indeed?' Mr Foxcroft said, sitting down himself where he could look at her.

'You must have expected me, Mr Foxcroft, do not deny it.'

'Oh, I shan't, believe me; but perhaps you could tell me just why I was to receive this delightful visit.'

Eliza drew herself up a little straighter. It would never do for her to look drab, although she could wish she might have found something a little less warm to wear than Lady Crawley's old furs. 'You must know, Mr Foxcroft,' she continued determinedly, 'that I have made Miss Crawley my legatee.'

'You have?'

Eliza nodded. 'When I die she will inherit some very sizeable property in Bedfordshire, besides some quite considerable amount safely in the Funds.'

Mr Foxcroft contemplated her dryly. 'I cannot see that it signifies, Miss Stanley, since when you die I shall doubtless be too antiquated to care!'

She flushed quickly and turned her head away. 'That is nonsense, as well you know. You cannot say it is a matter of disinterest to you!'

'I can't?'

Eliza felt suddenly incensed. His tone was that of someone listening politely to the most boring conversationalist and as she looked at him he raised one hand to smother a yawn. Her eyes flashed. If she had been determined before, she was more so now and Mr Foxcroft was rather startled when she rose and took several impatient steps towards him. 'Mr Foxcroft, I shall tell you, without roundaboutation, that your proposed marriage does not suit me. If I wished, I could make Sophia a very wealthy woman. However, I shall not stand idly by while the girl makes herself an alliance I can only consider disastrous and which will only serve to make the two of you as miserable as hell-cats.'

This speech moved Mr Foxcroft to stand up. His expression of boredom had flown, to be replaced at first by surprise and then by angry scorn. 'Surely, Miss Stanley, this is a matter purely for your niece and myself.'

'On the contrary. Lucius is a weak man, although he would never admit it. His sole desire is to see his daughter handsomely settled. I, however, have more than a passing interest in my niece's happiness. She is already quite distraught. How will she feel when her father's will and your own obstinacy have forced her into such an odious marriage of convenience?' She had not intended to say one half of this. Gone was Aunt Jemima, there instead was Eliza Woodeforde, determined against all the odds to rescue her darling from so hopeless a future.

Mr Foxcroft was frowning hard. He had seen the change, subtle though it was, and realized that, whoever this weird lady was, she was certainly sincere. Eliza was pacing the room now, the warmth and weight of the sables quite forgotten.

'It's a fine thing, isn't it, Mr Foxcroft, when a gentleman's wealth and influence can force an innocent like my Sophy into marriage. I should have thought, sir, that you would have known better than to propose to a girl barely out of the school-room, who has lived all her life in a Somersetshire manor and who knows no more than to obey her father's every command! Could you not see how wretched she has become? Or are you so blind to all but your own concerns that you are quite incapable of seeing anything?'

Mr Foxcroft did not speak. The strange woman before him had been pacing the room in an agitated manner, the sables swinging and flying behind her, the painful spectacles removed and twisted, disregardedly, between her fingers. Her cheeks were flushed and her eyes bright; Mr Foxcroft thought he had rarely seen a woman look so becoming. She stood before him now, her bosom heaving, giving him look for look, hardly noticing the vague suspicion of a smile that curled his lip. 'Well?' she demanded impatiently, turning and casting the innocent spectacles upon a small round table. 'Have you nothing at all to say?'

He contemplated her with amusement. 'Miss Stanley, what should I say? If Miss Crawley found my suit distasteful she could have apprised me of the fact. I hope I am not so unapproachable.'

She laughed without humour. 'To a child of eighteen, twenty years your junior? I should tell you, sir, that she considers you much as she would an aging uncle and even wonders if, like her father, you suffer from the gout!'

He was startled now and was betrayed into laughter. 'Did she indeed? How vastly diverting! However, she may rest easy, for I have never suffered anything more than a mild attack of influenza and that was when I was still in short trousers, many moons ago. You may tell her if you wish!'

'I shall tell her no such thing,' Eliza muttered, turning that he might not see the angry tears that had welled in her eyes. 'How can you be so unfeeling, Mr Foxcroft? Do you so desire my niece that you will marry in the face of her own distress?'

He raised his brows at the back of her head. 'Miss Stanley, I fail to comprehend you.'

'Mr Foxcroft,' she said, her voice like ice,

'you comprehend me very well! I may have lived the life of a recluse but the significance of your reputation has not been lost on me! You are a rake, sir. Even I know this! What can you want with my poor Sophy except to spite her for not responding to your advances? Indeed I cannot think how Sir Lucius was so blind that he could not see what you were about!'

Mr Foxcroft gave a startled laugh. 'You seriously think, Miss who-ever-you-are, that I would sacrifice my freedom simply because a chit from the school-room would not become my mistress? What ridiculous notions you cherish, ma'am!'

She stared up at him now, oblivious of the tear that stood upon her cheek. 'I am sorry for that. You must forgive me for saying such an unbecoming thing.'

Her eyes fell and she did not see the distinctly strange expression that had entered Mr Foxcroft's eyes. It was gone in a moment, however, so when she raised her own to his face again she saw him simply mildly amused.

'Miss Stanley, I forgive you, the Lord knows why! No woman has ever said such a thing to me before and earned my forgiveness!'

She flushed and moved away. 'Mr Foxcroft, won't you give up my little Sophy? I cannot believe your heart to be engaged or you would not talk so. This must be some fancy of yours, I cannot believe otherwise; and while you believed her complaisant, well, you could not be blamed. But now you know the truth, will you not withdraw?'

She turned huge, pleading eyes upon him, but he shook his head. 'Ma'am, I cannot. You speak as though any young woman would suffice. Well, that is not very flattering to your little Sophy, is it? Besides, I am by no means convinced of her antipathy to the match. She has given me no indication of it, I assure you!'

'Of course not!' she exclaimed, exasperated. 'She knows how overjoyed Sir Lucius is, how much he wants her to contract the alliance! The thought of disappointing him is loathsome to her!'

He was staring at her fixedly now. Gone was the angry young woman of a moment before and the solitary tear upon her cheek would have moved a sterner man than Mr Foxcroft. In a moment, however, he recollected himself and hardened his heart. Turning from her he searched for his snuff-box and said, casually: 'I shall not withdraw, Miss Stanley. It is a matter of indifference to me whether Miss Crawley is an heiress or a pauper. As for wishing to please her father, that is hardly a fault, but I suggest that you apply to him. Perhaps he will be more willing than I to listen to your case.'

Eliza was silent. He had his back to her, so she could not see his face, but she had the unpleasant sensation that she had somehow managed to amuse him. But his words were hard and his voice implacable. Turning, she gathered up Sophy's gloves and in a moment she had left the hotel.

For some little time she walked blindly, not noticing where her hasty steps were taking her. Moved at first by wrath this soon gave way to shame when she thought of what she had said to the unfortunate gentleman in question. It did not take long, however, for despair to replace this. She had played her trump card and all that remained now was for her to tackle Sir Lucius. But this had seemed quite pointless from the start. Deep in distraction, she wandered on through the Bath streets.

Sophia had been incredulous when Eliza had suggested the scheme. How could she possibly do such a thing? Was not Aunt Jemima over sixty and eccentric into the bargain? But Eliza had soon dispensed with these objections. Mr Foxcroft was not to know and, anyway, could she not have been her Mama's younger sister instead of her elder? Sophia had agreed, but reluctantly. However would Eliza convince him? She was so young, so pretty. It was quite impossible!

'I don't think so,' Eliza said thoughtfully. 'I can do my hair differently, you know, and put some flour on it to grey it slightly.'

'Flour!' repeated Sophy, giggling a little.

'Yes, and you shall find me your Mama's sables—I cannot think she would mind, can you, for this?—and perhaps the green pelisse?

I don't think I can wear my old brown, for he is sure to see where I was obliged to darn it the other day, and I cannot quite be satisfied that I have removed all the mud!'

Sophia shook her head, her eyes large, and gave her opinion that dear Mama would surely be happy to know she could help her daughter so long after her death.

'Precisely, my love,' concurred Miss Woodeforde, pleased. 'I think I shall wear my own black bonnet, for although it is quite outmoded that will be better, I think, than one of yours. Only, can you lend me some gloves?'

'Of course!' Sophy cried, springing up to look for them. The adventure, Eliza noticed, had returned some of the colour to her drawn little face.

They spent the evening rummaging through the old trunks in the attic, discovering, besides the sables and the green pelisse, still in good enough repair, Eliza noted, several other treasures Sophia had forgotten about. When she found the old spectacles her Mama had used to wear for her needlework she had cried out in delight. Eliza took them and tried them on, but the lenses hurt her eyes so much that she was obliged to take them off.

'You could knock out the glass,' Sophia suggested tentatively.

But Eliza shook her head. 'No, for he would surely see. I shall take them and wear them just a little, when he is looking at me

47

particularly closely.'

'Eliza, do you really think it will work?'

'I don't know, dearest, but what can we possibly lose? Even if he does find out, and there is no reason why he should, what can he possibly do?'

Sophia looked grave. 'Papa might dismiss you, Lizzy, if he finds out.'

'Well, that is a chance I must take.'

'Oh Eliza, I'm so grateful to you! You're so clever, I'm sure you will succeed!'

Well, she had not. Sophia's trust had been misplaced and her own judgement incorrect. It would seem Mr Foxcroft was not so fond of wealth that he ever craved for more.

In the lounge of the York House Hotel Mr Foxcroft stood for several moments surveying the empty chamber. It was true the lady had amused him; but she had fascinated and intrigued as well and he had realized that, in spite of the brown hair streaked spasmodically with grey, she was nowhere near as antiquated as she would have preferred him to believe. The impression that they had met before had been powerful from the start. It had troubled him throughout the interview; but it had only been when the fire of anger had lit up her eyes that recollection had come. Thoughtfully he picked up the discarded spectacles and twisted them between his fingers. Would she return for them, he wondered? He decided she would not, especially since she had not needed them.

He put them absently in an inside pocket and went to eat his meal. Upstairs in his chamber somewhat later, he found his valet in the action of laying out his evening-dress. He surveyed it with distaste and then sighed and permitted the round-faced Jameson to assist him from his coat. In spite of his amusement—and at the time this had been large—his visitor of the afternoon had delivered quite a shock. That Miss Crawley was averse to his proposal he had had no idea. To be sure, she had never offered him the least encouragement, but this he had attributed to her youth and inexperience and indeed he had been heartily glad of it. But, if she truly felt herself coerced, then there was only one thing he could do. When he thought of withdrawal, however, disinclination reared its awkward head. There was not one person he had told who had been pleased at his engagement; how delighted would they be on its dissolution! As he thought of his sister, his lip curled slightly, and his valet, the diplomatic Jameson, knew misgivings suddenly about the propriety of the waistcoat he had just then laid out. Mr Foxcroft was a man of reckless spirit, despite the homely tendencies besetting him of late. Consequently the thought of irritating his infuriating sister appealed to him considerably and he began to formulate a plan that would achieve this without causing the little Sophia any further heartache.

'Excuse me, sir, but what do you desire I should do with these?'

Jameson's carefully modulated tones cut unexpectedly through his thoughts. The valet, feeling, as was his custom, in the pockets of his master's coat before taking it to press, had found the ancient spectacles and now, with an expression of polite inquiry, held them out for his master's inspection.

But Mr Foxcroft grinned. He had forgotten for the moment his early evening visitor, but now she entered his thoughts again and he saw her as she had looked when she was so angry. She was not as pretty as Sophy, for she lacked that classic perfection of feature, and her mouth was too wide. But she was certainly striking, with eyes that pleaded one moment and flamed the next, and was possessed of a spirit he had not often seen. Had he not known for certain that Miss Crawley did possess such a relation he would have suspected it to be all a jest, an extravagant wager, perhaps at his expense. But the woman had been sincere. There was no denying this fact and he frowned again. He wondered if she could have been a cousin, or a more distant relation, but he rejected this thought. Cousin Susan he had met and a more disagreeable woman he had yet to encounter. Sophia herself had told him how few relations she had and in fact there had seemed to be only one person in her life, apart from her dear Papa, whom she had had any affection for.

At this thought Mr Foxcroft grinned. The missing governess-companion, whose absence Sophia had so bewailed, was away visiting some sick relative, or some such thing. Had she not said, many times within his hearing, that if Eliza were there she would know what to do? About what, he had not considered. Sophia spent so much of her time talking inanities that he had paid her very little heed, merely resolving to give her mind a more purposeful direction once the knot was tied. Had he listened, he might have discovered therein the reason for his visitor, and he cursed himself now for dismissing it all as a child's witless prattle. To be sure, they had been left very little alone. There had always been Lady Winterton or, more recently, the tallow-faced Miss March and, although at the time he had welcomed this, he was beginning to think now that it would have been wiser to have become better acquainted with Miss Crawley before so entangling himself. He sighed and allowed himself to be helped into his shirt. It would behove him to tread warily now; Sir Lucius had been so overjoyed at his proposal, so anxious to see the knot tied that he pondered on the extent of his fury should the engagement be dissolved. He would be quite capable, Mr Foxcroft felt, of taking him to court and, although this thought caused him some amusement, it might yet be a source of embarrassment for him and jubilation for his sister. He grimaced again and somewhat impatiently received his cravat from the valet.

Jameson was very silent. His master's mood, it was plain to see, was not conciliatory and he knew quite well that a chance word of his now would serve to throw his master into the boughs. He watched silently, therefore, as Mr Foxcroft made the intricate arrangement known as a Mathematical, shaking his head slightly when the arrangement proved to be unsatisfactory. He was all too familiar with such things. To be sure, Mr Foxcroft was by no means as particular a gentleman as one of Jameson's previous masters, a foppish young man who thought nothing of spending three hours on his toilet; but there had been times when a half dozen cravats would be required before the desired effect was quite achieved. He had known at once how it would be tonight. Of late his master's mood had been sunny enough, but the visit to the Metropolis had served to bring on one of his blue megrims and he foresaw difficulties ahead. After three attempts his master seemed satisfied, however, and Jameson laid aside the spare cravats to help his master on with his coat.

The following morning Mr Foxcroft slept late. He had lingered rather too long the previous evening over his port, as the events of the past weeks flooded back to disturb him. But the more he drank, the more confused his reasoning, until, although he knew he was not yet disguised, he realised he was not making rational decisions. He sought his couch therefore and slept soundly and late, to awaken with no recollection of anything at all. His memory returned soon enough, however, and he swung his feet to the floor with a feeling of pleasurable anticipation. He knew he ought by rights to drive out to Malham Park that morning, but for the moment he remained undecided about his course of action, so he arrayed himself for the Pump Room. It was not his habit to drink the waters; indeed, on the single occasion he had made the attempt to do so, he had found them quite disgusting and wondered at those persons who came to Bath for no other reason. But this was Bath's principal meeting-place and, since he could think of nothing more entertaining to do, he decided he would take a look at Bath's gentle-folk.

He found himself almost immediately hailed. Notable Corinthians like Mr Foxcroft were no longer as frequent visitors to Bath as they had been in Mr Nash's day and, since he had chosen to rig himself out that morning in the first style of elegance, with pantaloons of dove-grey and a coat of dark blue superfine with silver buttons, he could hardly escape notice. He had never been one to adopt the extremes of fashion; even in his youth he had frowned upon those members of the Dandy set whom nothing pleased better than to appear in coats with wasp waists and padded shoulders, and to array themselves with large quantities of fobs and seals and with cravats the height of which often made neck movement difficult. Mr Foxcroft's cravat was certainly complicated but it was not excessive, nor were the points of his shirt so high they reached his ears. No, it was his elegance, together with an air of calm authority that spoke of Town bronze, that attracted attention and when he found himself addressed he turned at once, his charming smile already curling his lips.

'So you have returned, Mr Foxcroft,' said the lady in question, an ample female with four chins who was rolling across the room towards him.

Mr Foxcroft bowed and kissed her hand. 'Lady Langdale! You are plainly quite recovered. I never saw you in better health!'

Lady Langdale flushed and beamed. 'Why, thank you, sir! I own I do feel much more the thing. But we missed you, Mr Foxcroft! I'm sure we all hoped, when we saw the announcement, that you would now be a *settled* visitor!'

'Well, so I hope to be, ma'am,' Mr Foxcroft said.

'Though I'm sure you find us all very dull work,' Lady Langdale pursued, barely listening to him. 'After London, I wonder that you can abide our slow ways! I'm sure I was never

54

more surprised to discover that you had so taken to one of our very own beauties!'

'Shame on you, Amelia!' exclaimed a middle-aged lady who had just then joined them. 'I'm sure you will put Mr Foxcroft quite to the blush with such phrases! Mr Foxcroft, it is a pleasure indeed! I hope your London business was successful.'

'Oh certainly, I thank you, but I was glad to return. One finds London life a trifle fast after a while!' He glanced around the room as he spoke, wondering how he was to escape these two voluble ladies without offending them. As they chattered on he saw, across the room, a tall, bony woman, her frame startlingly encased in a gentleman's black evening-cape with purple lining, and sporting on her head an old felt hat with a long, upstanding pheasant's feather. The sight was so extraordinary that it was a moment before he realized she was staring at him quite as intently as he was at her. He became aware that his two companions had ceased speaking and were indeed looking at him expectantly. He turned with a smile therefore and said easily: 'Forgive me! I believe I see an *old* acquaintance across the room!'

'For shame, Mr Foxcroft!' cried Lady Langdale with mock offence. 'Leaving us for greener pastures?'

'Let him go, Amelia, if he wants to,' Mrs Henry advised her friend bluntly. 'There's nothing worse, I know, than making someone feel they *must* remain! Go, Mr Foxcroft, but we charge you to return! We see too little of you in any event!'

He bowed and moved away and they watched as he approached the extraordinary-looking woman in black. 'Good heavens,' Lady Langdale exclaimed, 'is she his old friend? I declare I never saw a stranger-looking outfit! Surely, Louisa, that is a gentleman's cape?'

'I'm sure it is,' the other responded dryly, 'but there is no doubt but what it has achieved its purpose.'

'Good-morning,' Mr Foxcroft began, eyeing the elderly lady with some appreciation. 'We have not met, have we?'

'No, Mr Foxcroft, we have not,' she returned, eyeing him with a very straight eagle-stare, 'but I made it my business to find out who you were.'

'You did?'

'Most certainly. And, I must say, I had not expected to find such a Bond Street Beau!'

'A Bond Street Beau!' Perversely, the lady's direct manner amused him.

'Do you deny it, sir? I must admit, I have remained a recluse so many years I have quite lost touch with these modern fashions. But I am certain that in my day no gentleman would dare to appear in such . . . extraordinary items of dress as those!' She indicated with one bony forefinger his dove-grey pantaloons. 'However,

Mr Foxcroft, since I have not come to criticize your apparel, I will refrain and indeed,' she continued, throwing one spiked glance around the room, 'I can see a great many more worthy of criticism than you!'

'Madam, I am sure I should be gratified!'

'Well, you should, for I ain't mealy-mouthed, as you have discovered, I am sure, to your cost!'

His eyes held an amused twinkle. 'Madam, you intrigue me. *Have* we met?'

'Mr Foxcroft, do you think you would forget me if we had?'

He laughed now. 'Indeed no! But you appear to know a great deal more about me than I about you!'

'On the contrary, I know very little, though I have been told you are something of a loose fish. Indeed your reputation is such that even I have heard of you—though not in such terms as I have recently been apprised!'

He looked startled. 'Indeed, madam! May I ask what those are?'

'I have been told, Mr Foxcroft, that you have the reputation of a rake, that your consideration for the female race is not only non-existent, but it leads you very often to treat them in the most abominable fashion.' Her steady gaze pierced him. 'What have you to say to that?'

'Nothing, ma'am,' he replied, his lips twitching. 'You see me as I am, a man of the world, I do not deny it.'

'Which is just as well, for I have to tell you, sir, that I am Jemima Stanley.'

If she had hoped to discompose him she was disappointed. His lips twitched and he regarded her in a fascinated way before saying, amusedly: 'I'm sure you are, but can you offer any proof of that?'

'No, I cannot, but I know exactly who I am!'

He smiled now and said: 'Perhaps you can tell me, Miss Stanley, if these are your spectacles?'

Miss Stanley raised her thin, pencilled brows. 'Spectacles? Mr Foxcroft, I have never had the smallest need for aids of any kind. My vision is perfect and so is my hearing, as you will soon discover, if you should ever attempt to whisper about me.'

'Miss Stanley, I hope I shall never be so uncivil!'

'I hope not, but I do not place much dependence upon such things, particularly when dealing with a person described to me as a *hedgebird*, sir!'

He blinked and then laughed. 'Indeed, ma'am, I should like to know your source of information!'

'Undoubtedly you would, Mr Foxcroft! However, you may be easy, for I never make judgements except by my own findings!'

'In that case I find myself considerably eased, though I should inform you, if you are indeed Miss Stanley, that I have no intention of withdrawing from my engagement, whether Miss Crawley is a pauper or possessed of thirty thousand pounds.'

Miss Stanley considered him, her brown eyes as acute and piercing as a fox's. 'Vastly pretty, I am sure! However, I have very little interest in your preferences! As you seem to be aware, all I have will go to Sophia, but I shall not countenance a match I think unfit! I tell it to your head, sir, I cannot conceive what that clunch of a brother-in-law of mine was about in allowing it! As far as I can recollect, the child is barely eighteen, although I will concede my memory ain't what it was.'

'Your memory is not at fault, Miss Stanley. She is eighteen indeed.'

Jemima Stanley grunted. 'Then what are you about, sir, in taking up with a girl out of the school-room? I hope I am not such a simpleton as to think no London belle has ever set her cap at you!'

'Of course not. Which is why, Miss Stanley, when I met your niece I became convinced that she was just the wife for me.'

The fox eyes narrowed suddenly. 'It was your intention to become leg-shackled, Mr Foxcroft?'

He was not surprised to hear these cant terms on Miss Stanley's lips but he smiled nevertheless, saying: 'I admit, yes. Undoubtedly the stories you have heard are based on fact.

My chief desire was to change my style of life.'

'Bored you, did it? Well, that's no surprise. However, I'll not stand idly by while the chit makes a disastrous match of it. What proof is there that you won't return to your scapegrace ways in a month?'

Mr Foxcroft smiled. 'None, ma'am! What can I say? My intentions are good, though I dare say that means nought to you!'

'You are in the right of it, Mr Foxcroft! But you have a plain manner and I like that.'

'You honour me, ma'am,' the gentleman responded dryly. 'However, I do not give a fig for what you think.' He considered a moment. 'Do you know, Miss Stanley, that not one person connected with me has been cheered by my engagement? In fact I have even had a Miss Jemima Stanley at my hotel yesterday trying to dissuade me in the most obvious fashion!'

Miss Stanley contemplated him expressionlessly. 'Impossible. What humbug is this?'

'None, I assure you! I returned to Bath to find the lady awaiting me. Swathed in furs, ma'am, and sporting these!' He twirled the spectacles again and smiled at her.

Miss Stanley did not respond. She contemplated him a moment longer and then said: 'Mr Foxcroft, you will not gammon me, you may be sure! What did this person want?'

'My withdrawal, ma'am, like everyone else!'

60

'Indeed!' The brown eyes snapped suddenly. 'And she impersonated me to do it?'

He nodded, drawing out his snuff-box with an absent air. 'I have my own notions about it however.' Carelessly he flicked open his box and took a small pinch.

'Old Bureau?' Miss Stanley demanded, eyeing him with sudden interest.

He laughed. 'No, my own! King's Martinique, with a touch of Brazil, among other things!'

'Indeed! You mix your own snuff!'

'Yes, ma'am. Should you care to try?'

'Indeed I should. I am not impartial to it, I will admit.'

Without a flicker of surprise Mr Foxcroft held out the box, causing Lady Langdale to nudge her companion to observe the latest turn-up.

'She is certainly an original,' Mrs Henry remarked, interestedly. 'I wonder who she is? Mr Foxcroft seems quite amused.'

'But then he is so very charming, do you not think so?' Lady Langdale returned, glancing at her friend. 'I am sure he is far too well-bred to be impolite even to such an oddity as she is!'

'Fair and far out, Amelia! Mr Foxcroft is only charming because it pleases him to be so. I have heard him utter the most damning set-down you can imagine and, although it was certainly justified, the poor woman was vastly put out. Indeed she cannot now see him without blushing in the most unbecoming manner!'

'Truly?' Lady Langdale was fairly caught. 'Who was it, Louisa, do I know her?'

'Oh no, I am sure you do not,' came the infuriatingly cool response.

Lady Langdale stood silent for a moment before, overcome once more by curiosity, saying with nervous speed: 'Well, whoever that weird lady is she must be simply *steeped* in money! She would not otherwise have won over our Mr Foxcroft.'

'You forget,' Mrs Henry said dryly. 'He said she was an old friend.'

'So he did,' Lady Langdale agreed. 'How very odd!'

Across the room Mr Foxcroft was laughing. 'Where, ma'am, did you come to learn about snuff?'

'Where? It is one of my most engrossing pastimes, Mr Foxcroft—that and my dogs. But this!' She shook her head. 'Too much Macouba, sir, sure as check!'

'And you, ma'am? What do you use?'

She smiled sourly at him. 'You might one day so win my regard that I send you a jar. But part with my recipe I will not!'

'Very well, ma'am,' said Mr Foxcroft meekly. 'I shall look forward to that day!'

'Moonshine!' Miss Stanley told him roundly. 'And we wander, sir, from the object of our conversation. You shall not escape so lightly, you may be sure!'

'I hope, ma'am, that I should not attempt to do so. However,' he said, glancing about him, 'we are attracting not a little attention standing here. I wonder, should you care to try a glass of the waters? They are, I believe, generally considered beneficial.'

The sharp eyes dealt him one dagger glance. 'You feel I need it, I collect!'

'Not a bit, ma'am,' the gentleman responded cheerfully. 'However, it is not the thing to visit Bath and not try them though they are indeed quite vile! I have tried them myself,' he added, with a wry smile.

The old lady gave a barking laugh and said: 'Very well, lead me on! No one shall ever say Jemima Stanley was not game at every fence!'

Accordingly he escorted her across the room and she dutifully swallowed the glass of evil liquid. 'Vile, as you say,' she remarked, handing him the glass. 'We agree on one thing at least!'

'On more than one, ma'am,' Mr Foxcroft responded soberly, setting the glass aside. 'I too have no desire to see Miss Crawley make an unhappy alliance.'

She eyed him sharply. 'Strange words, sir, for the prospective bridegroom.'

He nodded. 'Your namesake, ma'am, I fear, is responsible.' He took a number of hasty steps and then said: 'Whoever she was, she was in no funning humour; of that I am convinced!

She told me Miss Crawley was vastly put out by my proposal and indeed had been made quite wretched by it! If this is indeed so, I shall certainly withdraw my suit.'

'Will you, indeed!' Miss Stanley had assumed an expression of thoughtfulness. 'Who was this strange female, Mr Foxcroft?'

He frowned. 'The governess, if I am any judge.'

'*Governess*? Sophia has no need, surely, for any such now?'

'No. She is more of a companion and a friend. I had not previously met her. At least,' he amended quickly, 'not to my knowledge, as she was away at the time on some errand of mercy.'

Miss Stanley smiled sourly. 'A governess with a position of advantage, it would seem!'

'Yes, indeed. Trusted greatly, I believe, by Miss Crawley.'

The old woman nodded slowly. 'You believe her concern for Miss Crawley prompted this— ludicrous charade? I could call it worse!'

'I do, but she was fine, to be sure!'

She raised her brows. A woman of no mean intelligence, she saw something that made her eyes narrow momentarily, but she said: 'Mr Foxcroft, are you a man of honour?'

'Miss Stanley, I hope so!' he responded, slightly startled.

'If Miss Crawley does not wish to marry you you will not enter into any contract with her

64

father?'

'Undoubtedly not,' he replied shortly, distaste showing in his face. 'In fact I intend to visit Miss Crawley about this, but she has a plaguey cousin with her who never leaves her alone!'

'Susan March,' Miss Stanley pronounced grimly. 'It was she who wrote to me.'

'Miss March?' For once, Mr Foxcroft looked surprised. 'I had not thought her an enemy, I must admit! Sour-faced and cross as crabs, but as keen to promote the match as Sir Lucius!'

'Fair and far out, I fear. She wrote me a fine tale about you, you may be sure! In fact,' she told him frankly, 'she had not a good word to say for you.'

A frown had creased Mr Foxcroft's brow. 'Miss Stanley, this is becoming a bore! Why should I not get married if I wish? What is it to Miss March in any event? It is no concern of hers.'

Miss Stanley afforded him her sour smile. 'Then you do not know the woman, sir. Her desire is to make her home with whoever will house her. Though she has a perfectly adequate income she is as cheese-paring as a parson and, having once wormed her way into Malham, she will take a parcel of digging out, I can tell you! As long as Miss Crawley remains unwed she may stay; but if she marries you, sure as check, Lucius will pack her off before she has time to catch her breath!'

'Hmmm.' Mr Foxcroft looked thoughtful. 'Miss Stanley, should you object to a little ruse? Nothing harmful, I assure you and I certainly shall not attempt it without Miss Crawley's consent!'

'Now what, pray, is in that devil-may-care head of yours? I'll not see my niece hurt, Mr Foxcroft, though I'll admit I've been careless enough myself until now! In fact I should not know her,' she conceded frankly.

'No, ma'am, on that head you may rest easy. But I have one or two scores of my own to settle,' he admitted, a faraway look entering his dark eyes.

'That's as maybe, Mr Foxcroft,' Miss Stanley pronounced sharply, causing him to jerk his head and look down at her. 'But what do you desire I should do?'

'Nothing, ma'am!' Mr Foxcroft grinned. 'Only do not betray me! Call it a crack-brained scheme if you choose, but I always had an odd kick in my gallop! Come to Ingham next week! I'll make no game of you, ma'am, you may rest easy; but there are those, ah, who amply deserve it!'

CHAPTER FOUR

Miss Woodeforde returned to Malham in deep thought. She had taken the carriage without permission, so she expected a sharp set-down, but it was not this that so occupied her, nor the reason for her brown study when she stepped absently onto the Malham drive. As she had expected, Sophia was there to greet her, hurrying down the steps with an anxious look that made Eliza feel a traitress. It was by now nearly dark and the girl took her companion's arm without a word and led her into the house. It was almost time for dinner, so, by silent consent, the two walked side by side up the wide stairway to Eliza's little chamber. Sophia perched on the bed. Eliza absently removed the pins from her bonnet, and then raised her eyes to her friend's face as she turned around.

'Sophy, I'm so sorry!'

Sophia sighed. 'Did he bubble you, Lizzy?'

She shook her head. 'I don't think so. At least,' here she paused thoughtfully, 'he did say he'd be too old to enjoy the money when I died, but I don't think—no, I'm sure he didn't. He just told me to take my case to your Papa.'

'Oh.' Sophia dropped her chin despondently. 'I was so certain you would succeed!'

'I know darling! I thought so too!' She

67

stepped out of her dress as she spoke and turned to take a grey cambric gown from the wardrobe. 'There is only one thing to do. I shall have to talk to your father.'

'No, Eliza.'

Miss Woodeforde paused in the action of stepping into her gown. 'No, Sophy? Whyever not? I thought it was what you wanted!'

'Yes, but—Oh Eliza, how can I do it to him? He would be so distressed with me and, besides, if I let you take my part in that way I should feel so ashamed! I should tell him myself if I really wanted him to know.'

'I see.' Contorting herself to fasten her gown, Eliza fell silent, but she was thinking as deeply as Sophia herself. 'Then you are resolved to marry him?'

'No! Oh, I don't know! Don't you understand, Eliza? If Mr Foxcroft had withdrawn his suit then perhaps Papa would not be *so* distressed!'

Eliza was forced to laugh. 'Dearest, what hubble-bubble notions you get! Do you truly think your Papa would want to see you miserable? How distressed do you suppose he would be if he found out after your wedding how much you hated it?'

Sophia sat silent. Sighing, Eliza began to brush her floury locks with something more than haste. Sophia had always had some decidedly odd notions in her top-loft, Eliza reflected. Indeed she had often herself called her pupil a delightful noddle-cock; but this: Eliza shook her head impatiently and began pinning up her hair in some haste. It was as well, she thought grimly, that no town beau ever thought to call on her of an evening! She would need to spend a great deal more than a mere five minutes on her toilet!

'Come on, Sophy,' she said to the girl, 'or you will really have me in the suds! It is nearly seven already!'

Indeed when they descended to the drawing-room they were greeted by an icy stare from Miss March and a heavy frown from Sir Lucius, who was only prevented from expressing his disapproval by Miss March's saying with chilling civility: 'Sophia! So you are come!'

'Yes, cousin. I have been talking with Eliza.'

'Indeed! And where has Miss Woodeforde been this day, might I ask? With the carriage too? I particularly desired to go shopping in Milsom Street, Sophia, and on your behalf, you may be sure, but what should I find but that the governess had taken the family carriage!'

'I asked her to go,' Miss Crawley responded suddenly, raising her chin and eyeing her cousin with unexpected frost. 'She was performing a particular errand, at my *express* desire, and besides,' here she threw an appealing glance at her father, 'she had Papa's permission.'

Sir Lucius sat grim and silent, his grey eyes hooded by the bushiness of his white eyebrows. Miss March gave a tittering laugh. 'He does not support you, I notice! Really, Sophia, you are becoming quite irresponsible these days! I'm sure I know not how you will go on at Ingham Place!'

'Hold your tongue, woman!' Sir Lucius growled. 'You forget yourself. You are not yet mistress at Malham! Miss Woodeforde went on an errand for my daughter, which should be enough for you! If you desire the use of a carriage I suggest you purchase one; you have funds enough.'

Cousin Susan's colour rushed up alarmingly, suffusing her face with a purplish hue from collar to hair-line. Whatever bitter retort hung on her lips she managed somehow to repress, saying in a voice of ice: 'Lucius, your suggestion might just be a valid one. Now, if we are all assembled I shall ring for Keen, provided, my dear friend, that you agree?'

She flashed her teeth at Sir Lucius but he did not respond, nor did he offer her his arm when he had dragged himself to his feet. Instead, and to Eliza's amazement, he bowed stiffly to Eliza herself and in a moment she found herself escorted to the dining-room. Whatever Cousin Susan's fury on this occasion, she managed somehow to repress it and even contrived throughout the extravagant repast that followed to maintain a light flow of conversation. The fact that no one else made the smallest push to assist her seemed to matter but little, and she laughed and sparkled on her own, ignoring the looks of pure loathing cast at her by her host and those of confused amazement by her cousin. Miss Woodeforde, although privately wondering at her mentality, yet kept her own counsel and addressed herself in silence, and without reaction, to her meal; but as the table was cleared of the various dishes she found her attention fairly caught, and that by a discussion of Miss Crawley's immediate future.

'I would you had not worn your primrose muslin again tonight,' Miss March was saying in her sharp way, smoothing her napkin with abrupt movements. 'When we go to Ingham you will need as many gowns as you can find and I see you have caught your slipper in your flounce yet again!'

'I have? Oh dear, when did I do that, I wonder?' Sophia had screwed herself around in her chair, peering at her skirt, but Sir Lucius had jerked up his shaggy head and directed a look of dislike at his niece. 'We? Surely, woman, you do not intend to go?'

She laughed shallowly. 'Why certainly, Lucius! What had you supposed? That I should permit her to go solely in your company? You invited me here to take care of the girl and that is what I propose to do.'

Sir Lucius growled. 'You are not going to

Ingham, Susan, so you may put that quite out of your mind. In fact,' he added consideringly, 'I think Miss Woodeforde will be company enough!'

'Miss Woodeforde?' Miss March gave a high-pitched laugh. 'Lucius, what are you thinking of? However will it look, may I ask, to have the future mistress of Ingham accompanied by none but her former governess?'

'A great deal better, you may rest assured, than if she were accompanied by such a plaguey sour-face as you are! I desire that she should show to advantage and with Eliza she will. It may have escaped your notice, and I'm certain you don't care to own it, but Miss Woodeforde has been more of a mother to my Sophy than anyone, particularly you! I had thought to go myself, but the journey and my gout make it out of the question.' He turned to his daughter. 'Speak, girl. What do you think of it as a scheme? Pretty well, eh?'

'Yes sir! I mean, it will be just the thing, if Eliza does not object.'

'Object? Nonsense! Why should she object? She'll be as merry as a grig, make no mistake! Though we'll have to see she's more up to snuff than *that*!' He pointed one twisted finger at Eliza's person, clothed as it was in grey cambric, and she blushed slightly. 'A fine turn-up it would be, miss, for you to be showing me up in such a fashion! You may have—five guineas, I think, to give yourself a trimmer look.'

'Papa!' Sophia exclaimed, breaking into startled laughter. 'That will not buy Lizzy a pair of gloves!'

'It won't?' Sir Lucius scowled heavily at his daughter. 'Well, if it doesn't I shall want to know why not! What does she wear, for the Lord's sake? The finest doeskin would not be more than a guinea, at most!'

Sophia giggled. 'Papa, it must be many years, then, since you bought anything! At least give Eliza ten guineas. That way I dare say she will be able to fashion something tolerable.'

'Well.' Sir Lucius obviously debated within himself. 'If she's to have a regular bang-up turn-out I suppose I must.'

'Lucius, I cannot but think this is most unwise!'

Sir Lucius Crawley growled. If anything were to serve to convince him of the wisdom of his actions it was his niece and he said sharply: 'Miss Woodeforde, come to me in my library after dinner and we'll see what can be done for you. I'll not have any dashed hanger-on telling me what I should or shouldn't do.'

Miss March forced a smile to her thin lips and murmured that such generosity was only what she had come to expect from her dearest uncle.

'How much did he eventually give you,

Eliza?' Sophia demanded eagerly when they were alone together.

'Ten guineas!' Eliza told her, her grey eyes twinkling in amusement. 'I'm sure I have Cousin Susan to thank, though she would hate to think it.'

Sophia giggled. 'I know, and she was as cross as crabs after you left! She had quite set her heart on going to Ingham, you know, which is why Papa won't allow it, I'm sure.'

'Sophy, you don't mind going just with me?' Eliza looked up somewhat anxiously.

'Of course not, you goose! Anyway, Papa asked me if I really wanted her to go, for he did not mean me to be more put out than I need, so what could I say? Besides, I do not believe he really trusts her out of his sight!'

'No,' Eliza agreed thoughtfully.

'The only thing is,' Sophia continued, 'it might be a trifle awkward if Mr Foxcroft should happen to recognise you.'

Eliza raised her chin. 'It cannot signify if he does and indeed it would please me enormously if he did!'

'Really?' Sophia eyed her friend dubiously. 'Well, if that is so, you are far braver than I! I'm sure I should never dare to meet him again after such an encounter as you had!'

'What can it possibly signify?' Eliza returned, somewhat crossly. 'Though I posed as someone else my sentiments were honest and so I shall tell him if I ever get the

74

opportunity.'

It seemed the next day as though Eliza would have the opportunity before she realized. Mr Foxcroft, having acquired an animal, hacked out to Malham Park in the early afternoon and surprised the whole household by his sudden appearance. Miss March, engaged in pruning Sir Lucius's roses, was privileged to see him first and hurried in to apprise her young cousin of her good fortune. Sophia was kneeling on the floor in the drawing-room where she had been busy reading *Angelina's Promise*, a novel, which she had secretly acquired from a circulating library through the agency of one of the housemaids. Her cousin's abrupt entrance startled her, but fortunately Miss March noticed only the state of her gown and not the book that protruded from behind her back.

'Really, Sophia, I wonder sometimes how I am ever to make a lady of you when you behave in such a hoydenish manner! Where is Miss Woodeforde?'

'She is out, cousin, walking. She said this morning that she had the headache.'

'Humph. Then I had better remain here. It will not be fitting for you to be left alone with the gentleman.'

'No, cousin, if you say not.' Sophia had seated herself demurely on the sofa and now contrived to stuff the forbidden novel behind one of its cushions. Her nervousness over the visit of her betrothed could not quite eclipse the fear she had lest her favourite pastime ever be discovered by her papa.

When Mr Foxcroft entered the room Sophia barely looked at him and therefore did not notice the rapid glance he cast about the room and the expression of disappointment that followed it. He bowed to Miss March and to her and then greatly disconcerted her by saying abruptly: 'Miss Crawley, do you care to take a turn in the garden? I have something I wish particularly to discuss.'

'A reasonable plan, Mr Foxcroft,' Cousin Susan said with her thin smile. 'Sophia, you had better fetch your wrap, for it is a trifle cold. I have left mine in the hall, I believe. Would you be so good as to bring it for me?'

'There will be no need,' Mr Foxcroft said, smiling charmingly. 'I shall accompany Miss Crawley.'

Miss March smiled again. 'Sir, I can understand your eagerness and Miss Crawley, I am sure, finds it most flattering, but it is hardly proper! I think it will be best if I come with you.'

'Madam,' Mr Foxcroft said sweetly, 'Miss Crawley and I are engaged! There can be nothing improper in a turn about the garden, and I will undertake to keep your young cousin well within sight of this window!'

'Oh, Mr Foxcroft,' cried Miss March, laughing, 'how droll, to be sure! Now, Sophia, be a good girl and fetch my wrap.'

'Miss March, I particularly wish to be private with Miss Crawley as there is something particular I wish to say out of your hearing. We have her father's consent; perhaps you also intend to be present on our wedding-night?'

Cousin Susan turned deep puce. While she wrestled within herself for a suitable reply Mr Foxcroft calmly escorted his betrothed from the room and shut the door.

'I hope you will forgive me for my bluntness,' he said in a low voice as they walked quickly towards the stairs, 'but she really is a most insufferable woman, even if she is your cousin!'

'Oh yes!' Sophia concurred, giggling nervously. 'She is always that way, I fear!' She left him then, hurrying away up the stairs, but as she forgot to raise the hem of her gown she caught her foot in it, falling heavily to her knees. Mr Foxcroft was beside her in a moment, solicitously helping her to her feet and asking if she were hurt.

'No, no! So stupid! My gown, it is too long! So stupid!' She hurried away then, having contrived to foil her betrothed's attempt to see into her face. He retraced his steps thoughtfully and then stood awaiting her in the hall. She returned some minutes later, her little face pale, and as he smiled at her he noticed the wide-eyed, apprehensive glance she cast him and wondered how he could ever have been so stupid as to miss it before.

It was quite mild outside, although it was only February, but Miss Crawley pulled her wrap tightly about her shoulders; but somehow she managed to get it tangled behind her and so was obliged to allow Mr Foxcroft to release it, a task he performed quietly, earning a quick look of thanks.

'Perhaps, Miss Crawley, we should take a turn in the shrubbery? I know I promised Miss March we would stay within sight of the window, but I do find her expression quite unnerving, do not you?'

Sophia glanced over her shoulder and laughed. 'She will probably follow us, you know,' she told him, far less self-consciously. 'She cannot bear not to know what is going on!'

'If she does she will contract pneumonia,' Mr Foxcroft replied, smiling. 'I bade that young fellow of yours to hide her wrap where it will take her all day to find it.'

'Young fellow? Oh, you mean Freddie, the footman? How clever of you! She will be as cross as crabs, you know, when she finds out.'

He glanced quickly at her. 'Shall you be in the suds over it? I should not have done it had I thought so!'

'Oh no! And it does not signify if I am. I think it a very good jest!'

They had gained the shrubbery by this time

and Mr Foxcroft, who prided himself on his ability to set people at their ease when he chose, felt a little dampened when Sophia turned large, anxious eyes upon him and said: 'Sir, you said you had something particular you wished to discuss?'

'I have, yes.' He would not have chosen to broach the subject so directly, but Miss Crawley had stopped in her tracks and now turned to face him, expectancy in her eyes. 'Shall we walk on a little, Sophia? It is not cold, but I should not like you to get a chill.' She turned obediently and they walked on, but Mr Foxcroft could not really congratulate himself on his handling of the matter. 'Miss Crawley, do you know I had a visitor yesterday?'

Her eyes flew to his face and she paled a little. 'Did you? No, I did not know.'

'Yes, indeed. It was your aunt, Miss Stanley. Do you know, she is a most charming lady?'

'No, I . . . no! That is, I do not know her, at least, hardly at all!'

'I see,' he responded gravely, sternly repressing his twitching lip. 'That was not the impression she gave me. In fact she seemed quite conversant with your sentiments.'

'With my—oh.'

She was looking straight ahead and, try as he would, he could not get her to look at him. 'Miss Crawley, I have been wondering—the fact is, I think I might have been a little premature. You see,' here he stopped and assumed an expression of awkwardness, 'in my haste to win your hand I think I might perhaps have overlooked something. After all,' he continued, smiling and moving on again, 'this is the nineteenth century, is it not! What I am trying to say, Miss Crawley, is that I think perhaps we should have a rather longer engagement than was at first planned. I cannot but think we would both benefit from knowing each other a little better. Do you not agree?'

Miss Crawley was walking aimlessly, rather agitatedly twisting the end of her wrap in nervous fingers. 'Oh yes! That is . . . oh dear! What I mean is,' Sophia said, controlling herself with a huge effort, 'that is a very good idea! I was a *little* anxious that the wedding should be quite so soon!'

'Good!' he said, smiling warmly on her. 'And I shall tell your father, so you shall have nothing to fear from that quarter!'

Sophia smiled gratefully up at him, leaving Mr Foxcroft to reflect ruefully on just what it had taken to make her look at him that way.

'You will of course come to Ingham next week?' Mr Foxcroft said, smiling down at her. 'I have asked my mother to come and she does desire most particularly to meet you!'

'Oh!' Sophia's cheerful expression faltered momentarily and then she said bravely: 'That will be nice! Will there be—a great many of your relations there, sir?'

'Only my mother,' he responded, 'but there will be another guest, you know.' She looked an inquiry and he replied, a smile twitching on his lips: 'Your Aunt Jemima, Miss Crawley! Did I not tell you I had met her? A most charming lady! Do you know she takes snuff?'

'Snuff? Oh, I am sure she does not! That is, how did you know she would be there?'

He laughed now. 'My dear Miss Crawley, I invited her myself, this morning, in the Pump Room.'

'In the Pump—oh, but there is Eliza now!'

If he had needed confirmation this artless declaration would have provided it. Miss Woodeforde, wearing a gown of faded lilac, was walking briskly towards the house and seemed not to have seen them. At the last moment she turned her head and paused. Mr Foxcroft thought she would have entered the house, but Sophia called out and she had no option but to join them.

'Eliza! How glad I am you are come! This is Mr Foxcroft,' she added, belatedly remembering that they had supposedly not met.

'How do you do, Miss Woodeforde,' Mr Foxcroft said, ignoring the inadequacy of the introduction and bowing. 'I hope I find you well!'

Eliza considered him. There was, she decided, an extremely wicked twinkle in his dark eye, but it was gone in an instant and she held out her hand. 'Thank you, I am very well. Have you been in the shrubbery? It is quite the wrong time of year, you know, to walk there. It can never be seen at its best until June.'

Sophia stared. There was something almost rude in Eliza's manner, but when she glanced at Mr Foxcroft she saw an appreciative gleam in his eyes that only served to perplex her further.

'I hear you are to join us at Ingham Place,' Mr Foxcroft said smoothly as they fell into step again.

'Oh, but I did not—that is—' Sophia stopped and looked at Eliza for guidance.

'Quite correct, Mr Foxcroft,' she responded calmly, ignoring her charge. 'How astute of you to find it out!'

'Not at all!' he responded, smiling wickedly. 'You are the most natural choice of course!'

Eliza bowed, but Sophia, out of her depth, said nervously: 'Indeed I said nothing! I cannot understand how—'

'Your father doubtless told him,' Miss Woodeforde replied, turning cool grey eyes upon the gentleman. 'Is that not so, sir.'

'Oh, most certainly,' he agreed promptly, his face and tone grave.

'Sophia,' Eliza said suddenly, 'I wonder, would you take this to Mrs Wainwright?' She held out the package she had been carrying. 'I called on Mrs Jervis in the gatehouse on my way home and she gave me a currant tart. If

82

Mrs Wainwright knows, we may have it tonight, I think, and you know how your father enjoys it.'

Sophia responded with alacrity. While alone with Mr Foxcroft she had been able, at least, to converse with him, but with Eliza present, although indeed she offered considerable protection, she felt quite lost amid the quick-fire exchanges they had indulged in. She took the tart therefore, bestowed a dazzling smile on Mr Foxcroft and ran into the house. Watching her, Eliza wondered that he could not see the child that yet remained.

'You should not tease her, you know,' Eliza said in her blunt way. 'She does not understand you, you see, and it upsets her.'

'I am sorry,' Mr Foxcroft said meekly. 'It was the sight of you without your spectacles. I found it hard to resist.'

'Well, you had better learn to try, sir,' she told him sternly, 'since we are to spend as much as a week in the same company! Or perhaps,' she added, turning on him with a sudden smile, 'you make it your business not to associate with governesses?'

'Undoubtedly,' he agreed solemnly. 'However, you may be easy. As Sophia's wealthy aunt you will doubtless attract a considerable amount of my attention. I should not like, you know, to see poor Miss Crawley cut off because of any laxity of mine.'

Miss Woodeforde eyed him fulminatingly.

'Cut line, Mr Foxcroft, if you please! This style of talk is no doubt vastly diverting to you, but it is not so to me and although I admit I might deserve your scorn my sentiments were honourable and they are unchanged.'

'So I should hope, Miss Woodeforde,' the gentleman responded, grinning. 'I should not like to see you turn so easily from your convictions!'

'And neither shall I, of that you may be sure!'

Mr Foxcroft considered her a moment, his head to one side. 'You are my enemy then, ma'am, sworn?'

She returned his look with a considering one of her own. 'No, sir, I am not that! I allow your feelings might have carried you away; but a man of honour, sir, you must admit, would not continue in this folly! Now you have seen how it truly is, you must surely withdraw!'

'But, ma'am,' Mr Foxcroft replied, smiling infuriatingly, 'I am not at all convinced of its folly! Indeed it has seemed to me, and on more than one occasion, that Miss Crawley is far from averse to my suit! You cannot surely have failed to mark how she regarded me just now?'

Eliza had not and she continued by his side for some minutes in silence. 'Mr Foxcroft, if you are correct, and I allow, I might have exaggerated the case, then there is no reason why you should not marry in time. But, sir, for

Sophia's sake, desist in your attempts for an early alliance! Let her at least come to know you a little and your ways!'

'Ah, ma'am, if only I could!' He shook his head and eyed her dolefully. 'It is, to be sure, a merry scheme! But Time, as you have yourself pointed out to me, is not on my side! I am eight and thirty, as I am sure you know. Forgive me, then, for being anxious to call my little Sophy my own! I have my name to perpetuate, you must know! For my father's sake this name of Foxcroft must live on and I shall need several sturdy sons within the next few years! And then too, consider, Miss Woodeforde, the other danger of a lengthy engagement. Miss Crawley might, after all, find me quite repugnant and then what should I do? At my time of life, you know, it is not easy to find damsels willing to wed one as decrepit as I. Who knows, if I allowed time, as you ask, some other, far more eligible, far more youthful gentleman might well capture her heart! And then, Miss Woodeforde, where should I be but jilted?'

Eliza had listened to this speech in mounting anger and indignation. Mr Foxcroft, it seemed, not only embodied the qualities she most despised in a gentleman, namely, inconsideration and scorn for the fairer sex, but he was also possessed of a most untimely sense of humour, making her feel, as she told herself, quite incensed. That he could talk so lightly about her Sophia's future she found intolerable; it had not escaped her notice that he seemed no more attached to her than he would have been to any young, presentable female who had happened to be in his neighbourhood at the time. When she felt herself to be in command of herself she summoned a stiff smile to her lips and said with forced calm: 'I am glad you find us such a source of amusement, Mr Foxcroft! I am sure we should feel flattered, but indeed I cannot find it in my heart to be so!'

He glanced sharply at her, for the last part of this speech had been uttered quite differently from the first. He said lightly however: 'Ma'am, it is I who should be flattered! Never in my life have so many persons taken such an interest in my future!' She glanced interrogatively at him and he said with a grim smile: 'Oh yes! My mother and sister would be heartily in agreement with you, to say nothing of my mistress! She, more than the others, I fear, was quite dreadfully put out!'

He had thought to shock her, but he failed, for she looked up at him now with an expression he found hard to fathom. All she said was: 'No woman likes to be supplanted, you should know!'

He laughed. 'Better than any man, Miss Woodeforde! If only I could feel it were for myself however.' He frowned momentarily and then said: 'No, that is unfair. My mother, at least, is disinterested.'

'She yet lives?'

He nodded. 'In London most of the year, though she spends a few weeks at Ingham. She is not strong.'

'Do you know, sir,' Miss Woodeforde said thoughtfully, 'I believe my father was acquainted with her, oh, many years ago. Is it possible?'

He shrugged. 'I cannot say, though I should have imagined her to be many years his senior. Who was your father?'

'Clarence Woodeforde, but my uncle is Lord Carlow, the Earl of Stiperden.'

'A Carlow Woodeforde?' He seemed astonished and stared at her in disbelief. 'How can that be?' he demanded.

Eliza smiled. 'He was disinherited, you know! It is quite common, I believe, and persists, even to this day!'

He smiled in return, but said: 'Does your uncle know what you do?'

'Of course,' she replied, raising her chin a little, 'though he takes care no one else does! We are very much the black sheep, I fear, though my sister, Agnes, Lady Marchmont, is acknowledged.'

He was silent for a moment and when he spoke again it was on an indifferent topic.

Sophia was waiting in the drawing-room for her friend's return. She had observed them for some little time from the window and since she knew they could have no other topic of conversation than her she had become not a little unnerved by the time they turned and made their way to the house. She noticed at once that neither was looking very happy, but that Eliza in particular was thoughtful. For a moment she wondered if they might both join her, but she soon heard Eliza's quick tread in the passage and rose in expectation. The door opened and admitted Eliza, looking just as thoughtful as before.

'Lizzy, whatever did he say? Did he recognise you?'

'Hmm? Oh yes! I feel he knew from the beginning how it was.'

'He knew! Oh, Eliza, how dreadful for you! Whatever shall you do?'

Miss Woodeforde looked with slight irritation at her charge. 'Do? What should I do, Sophy? I dare say he thought it a very good joke. He certainly seems amused!'

'A joke? He did not, then, tell Papa?'

Eliza shrugged. 'I'm sure I do not care if he does! What can it signify? Your Papa can only dismiss me and when you are married there will be no need for me in any event.'

'But—did he not tell you?'

'Tell me what?' Eliza demanded, turning impatient eyes upon the girl.

'About the engagement! I made sure he would tell you straight away! How strange he is!'

'I'm sure I know not! But what is it about the engagement, Sophy? What is it he has not told me?'

'That we are not to be married so soon! Oh, we are still engaged of course, that is not altered, but he says it will be better perhaps if we delay a little, which does sound as though he might be changing his mind. Do you think he is, Eliza? Do you?'

'A *long* engagement?' Eliza was eyeing the girl with a very strange expression in her grey eyes. Sophia, who had not seen it before, stared open-mouthed. 'Tell me, Sophy, did he suggest it himself?'

'Oh yes! And I wasn't expecting it at all! Really, he was very nice about it, I almost liked him today.'

'Almost—You mean you don't even *like* him?' Eliza exclaimed, astonished.

'Well, he is so very strange, is he not? He has such a way of looking at me, that makes me feel I have just been very droll, only I have not, Eliza, truly! And then he talks so oddly sometimes indeed I find it hard to comprehend him! Do you not think him odd?'

'I think him perfectly odious!' declared Miss Woodeforde with sudden venom. 'To think that all the time he was simply roasting me! Oh, it is infamous!'

'Eliza!' Sophia came to her anxiously and laid a hand upon her lilac sleeve but Eliza pushed it off impatiently and paced the room with angry steps.

'To say such things too! Oh, I knew he was laughing at me then, but this! It is intolerable!' She became aware of Sophia's staring at her in amazement and gave a shaky laugh. 'Forgive me, only you did not hear him, Sophy!'

'Was it very dreadful?' she asked, her ready sympathy aroused.

'Dreadful?' Eliza seemed surprised. 'No, no! If I had not been so angry I should have laughed!' She smiled at Miss Crawley. 'Forgive me! Have you never seen my temper before? No, I suppose you haven't, for I've been very good, haven't I? Papa used to despair of my ever catching a husband, such a shrew as I was, forever flying into the boughs!' She smiled reminiscently, but then recollected herself and said briskly: 'And he was quite right, wasn't he! But you have the temper of an angel. I only wish, with my whole heart, that you might find someone to appreciate it.'

Sophia eyed her wonderingly.

Sir Lucius Crawley eyed his prospective son-in-law with something less than pleasure. He had greeted Mr Foxcroft with rather less disdain than was usual, but this sunny humour had rapidly dissolved on hearing what 'the young coxcomb' had been plotting with his daughter. To Sir Lucius the most important thing in his life at that moment was the wedding of his only child. Having invited a despised relative beneath his roof it was now his prime object to be rid of her again and with this in mind an early date was the obvious answer. That the young renegade, so far from endorsing this view, should actually propose delay and have it accepted seemed the action of a traitor and he told the fellow so in no uncertain terms.

'Having second thoughts, are you? Well, let me tell you, sir, I'll have none of that with my daughter! She's a delicately nurtured girl, my Sophia, none of your rackety females, I've seen to that, and I tell you to your head, sir, that any ramshackle treatment from you will be badly received, very badly indeed!'

He followed this peroration with a threatening grunt, but Mr Foxcroft, so far from being unnerved, merely crossed one elegantly booted leg over the other and contemplated his future father-in-law with an unwavering eye. 'I have no intention of withdrawing,' he responded coolly, 'but such haste must look a little strange, must it not? Indeed I had thought the scheme rather would have pleased you.'

'Then you thought wrong!' shouted Sir Lucius, his niece uppermost in his mind. 'I want to see my daughter married and that I most certainly shall!'

'Of course,' the gentleman returned, still unflustered. 'We have altered nothing, but it suits both of us to delay a little longer. Your daughter is, sir, barely eighteen!'

'I had not forgot, Foxcroft!' Sir Lucius barked, growing rather red in the face. 'But you will marry my daughter, or I shall see you in court!'

'I have every intention of marrying Sophia, and she me, but I do feel it incumbent upon me to allow her a little time to adjust her feelings. When she has seen Ingham she will better understand what is in store.'

Sir Lucius was silent. His fear now was when Sophia saw the size and awesomeness of Ingham Place she would withdraw herself and he foresaw years with Susan at his dinner-table, supervising his servants and running his life. But then too he had to admit that Mr Foxcroft had been in the right of it and, since he had, under his grim exterior, a soft heart where his daughter was concerned, he could not but admit that his little Sophia would benefit from a little prior knowledge.

'Humph,' he said, regarding Mr Foxcroft dourly from beneath his brows. 'But what the devil am I to do with that plaguey female?'

Mr Foxcroft smiled. 'Miss Woodeforde, sir?'

'Devil a bit! Eliza's fair enough, though I grant you I never could abide a female with a mind of her own! Never been broke to bridle, that's her trouble, not but what her uncle's an Earl! But that's neither here nor there. I mean the other one, that cursed niece of mine! How shall I rid myself of her, tell me that, if my

Sophy be not wed?'

'I have a suggestion, sir, if you will permit me.'

'Of course, of course, but give it to me without roundaboutation, if you please!'

Mr Foxcroft smiled. 'If I were you, sir, I should pack up all her bags and order her carriage. If she does not go you may simply dispatch her possessions ahead of her and see how she will manage without.'

Sir Lucius gave a bark of laughter. 'Dammit, sir, you are a man after my own heart!' he exclaimed, a glimmer of approval in his grim eye.

'Oh, I should, sir,' Mr Foxcroft suggested, smiling very slightly. 'If you do not I fear she will be here next Michaelmas!'

The old man grunted. 'You're right, sir, burn it! The woman's a danged parasite! I must have had a screw loose when I invited her!'

'You were thinking of your daughter, sir, I am sure, but now Miss Woodeforde is returned she is hardly needed.'

'She ain't!' Sir Lucius agreed. 'Not the least particle of use. Never was! Mark me, Foxcroft, if I don't rid us of her first thing tomorrow!'

And so he did. Cousin Susan, returning to her chamber after breakfast, was astonished to find it utterly denuded of anything but the furniture. Hastening from the room she had presented herself, a raging virago, in her

uncle's study, but it had availed her little. Sir
Lucius, a most satisfied expression on his
furrowed face, permitted her to rage as she
wished and when she stopped for breath told
her without emotion that his carriage would be
ready within a half hour to take her where she
wished, although he suggested her apartments
at Wells, since her baggage had departed
thither a half hour since.

CHAPTER FIVE

A Foxcroft of Ingham! thought Eliza as the
carriage swung in at the impressively tall
wrought-iron gates. It was a conquest not to be
sneered at, even though the present owner of
this noble pile had proved himself so
unworthy. For it was certainly splendid. The
drive wound its way intriguingly through dense
woods through which, since the trees were yet
leafless, could be caught tantalising glimpses
of the house beyond. When it burst upon them
Eliza drew in breath. No wonder Cousin Susan
had impressed upon her young relation the
grandeur of Ingham. It lay, proud and regal,
before them and Eliza knew at a glance that
the tales of twelve miles of corridor could not
be fabrication. It was a Jacobean mansion and
utterly lovely. Dwarfing Malham Park, a fair-
sized manor built in the reign of German

George, it made the square elegance of that house look awkward and ugly. The roofs sloped away in a multitude of directions and angles. Surmounting them was a forest of chimneys and Eliza had a vague notion that every one would prove to be fashioned differently. While she was awe-struck she was not daunted, but Sophia, instead of exclaiming in delight and wonder as the carriage drew near, sat very still and silent.

The noise of their arrival had produced a liveried footman and in a moment their host himself. While the footman held open the door Mr Foxcroft helped the ladies to alight, bestowing on them impartially a flash of his famous smile. Civility required her to respond, but Eliza's reply to his polite inquiries was decidedly chilly, causing even the distracted Sophia to glance at her in surprise. But Mr Foxcroft seemed quite undaunted. He smiled in the face of her coldness, inquiring solicitously after her health and hoping she was not too wearied by the drive into Berkshire.

'Oh no, no!' exclaimed Sophia, aghast at the fact that her usually correct governess seemed about to give her host the cut direct. 'Indeed it has been most easy, has it not, Eliza? With the weather being fine, I declare it was even quite pleasant!'

Mr Foxcroft smiled at his betrothed. 'You enjoy travelling, Miss Crawley?' he said, as they moved towards the house.

'Oh yes! I do it so seldom, you see, except to Bath of course, but that is hardly travelling, as it is only three miles, isn't it, Eliza?'

Miss Woodeforde smothered a yawn. 'Indeed I have no notion, I'm sure! I find all travelling so dreadfully tedious!'

'Then you will doubtless wish to retire directly to your chamber,' responded Mr Foxcroft gravely. 'I will bid my housekeeper prepare you some gruel. At our age, you know, we cannot be too careful.'

Miss Crawley stared at him, but Eliza, whose face had previously been a study of boredom, was startled into laughter and threw him a glance of pure appreciation.

They were in the hall by this time, a chamber that proved to deserve that name, being, Eliza judged quickly, at least forty feet long. Her critical eye soon determined the minstrel's gallery at one end, together with the excellence of the carving that adorned it, and then fell with appreciation on the enormous log fire blazing almost insignificantly in the wide mouth of the fire-place.

'I hope you will forgive my mother for not being here to greet you,' Mr Foxcroft said, signalling to a liveried footman, 'but she suffers from a complaint that makes movement difficult. When you are refreshed I shall conduct you to her drawing-room, but first, your chambers.' He turned as he spoke, to converse in a muffled undertone with the footman, who then hurried away through one of the arched doorways that surrounded the hall.

A large stairway carved in oak swept upwards before them polished, Eliza noticed, with considerable care. After her desperate attempts at conversation Sophia had fallen silent again, but Mr Foxcroft was equal to anything, it seemed, and subjected them to a flow of trivia all the way to the first floor.

Mr Foxcroft had chosen, with, Eliza supposed, rare sensitivity, to position them not far from this central staircase. A fear had arisen in Miss Woodeforde that they would find themselves in one of the distant wings, which would not have discomposed her but which might well have disturbed Sophy. The chambers they were allotted were neither overlarge nor far removed from each other. In fact Eliza found herself in the rather larger of the two and silently applauded the gentleman's consideration. It seemed likely Miss Crawley would be overawed without any help of his. Their luggage had already been deposited and Eliza was just helping Sophia with her bonnet when there was a discreet scratching at the door. Mr Foxcroft, it would seem, was an observant and thoughtful host. A young housemaid appeared, her cap and apron snowy, with the purpose, it transpired, of operating as Miss Crawley's abigail. A moment's hesitation decided Miss Woode-forde to accept this, but when she found a similar person in her own chamber she made haste to dismiss her. She had never been waited upon in her life and, although she could appreciate Mr Foxcroft's consideration, she had no wish for her darned undergarments to be discussed at length in the servants' hall. She performed her own toilet at speed, changing, since it was past six, into her newly-fashioned evening-gown, which she had made in the late hours of the past few nights. Time being short she had fashioned it as simply as possible, but since she felt it became her situation not to be ostentatious she could not feel this to be a fault. As it was, the amber crêpe suited her to admiration and since she had always had a discerning eye as well as clever fingers the result could not be improved upon. She had hesitated for some time on her hair, finally rejecting the severe style she had adopted of late. For some unknown reason she decided on a soft arrangement she had often used for Sophy and could not but think the result rather fetching. She told herself she wanted to look well for Mrs Foxcroft, recollecting that she had been a great belle in her day, with an eye for the becoming. Besides, she told herself unnecessarily, she owed it to Sophia to look well.

She found Miss Crawley almost ready and had to admit that, for a housemaid, the young girl Foxcroft had sent certainly knew her business. She thought she had never seen Sophia look prettier, owning to herself reluctantly that much was owed to Miss Susan March's uncanny eye for a fetching gown. Sophia looked up nervously as Eliza entered, saying as the maid left:

'Eliza, you look well indeed! Is that your new crêpe?'

'Yes, but never mind about me! You look very pretty, Sophy, but you are so pale! Do you feel ill?'

Sophia shook her head. 'No, but, oh, Eliza, I am so frightened of meeting Mrs Foxcroft! I hear she is quite fearfully stiff-backed! Cousin Susan says she is so proud she cannot possibly like me!'

'What moonshine!' Eliza said, considerably annoyed with the absent Miss March. 'She was certainly a great belle in her day, I have heard that, and came from one of the best families, but I know nothing that says she is not perfectly amiable.'

Sophia did not answer, but a frown puckered her brow as she rose and left the room.

The drawing-room was large, but not overwhelming. Greeted by an impression of elegance and not oppressive grandeur Sophia relaxed a little, looking about her, and not immediately espying the shrunken figure in the wing-chair. When Mr Foxcroft came forward out of the shadows she started and turned her wide-eyed gaze upon the old woman he had been speaking to.

'Mama, this is Sophia, Miss Crawley.' He smiled encouragingly on her but she came forward nervously and only after some hesitation curtseyed and extended one small hand.

'How do you do!' smiled Mrs Foxcroft from deep within her chair. 'I have been so longing to meet you!'

'How do you do!' Sophia responded, thinking as she did so how thin and small Mr Foxcroft's mother was. The large chair dwarfed her, sunken as she seemed to be within herself.

'You must forgive me for not rising,' Mrs Foxcroft was saying, 'but I have such a stupid complaint!'

Sophia murmured something unintelligible and Mr Foxcroft stepped forward, saying: 'Mama, this is Miss Woodeforde, Miss Crawley's friend.'

Mrs Foxcroft turned deep eyes upon Eliza, forcing herself to look away from the strange expression on her son's face.

'Miss Woodeforde is one of the Carlow Woodefordes!' Mr Foxcroft added with a twinkle in his eyes. 'She believes you might have known her father.'

Mrs Foxcroft frowned momentarily. 'Your father, my dear? I don't think I recall—'

'I am probably mistaken, ma'am,' Miss Woodeforde said, smiling and stepping forward. 'I had some fanciful notion that it was so but it probably was not!'

'Tell me, my dear, who was your father?'

'Clarence Woodeforde, ma'am. My uncle is the Earl of Stiperden.'

'Clarence!' Mrs Foxcroft exclaimed. 'Oh yes, I do recall! Such a foolhardy young man, I remember. But no doubt he grew into a perfectly worthy gentleman.'

'He was sent to India, ma'am, and the family always preferred to pretend he didn't exist.'

'Oh dear! Well, I must admit I had heard something of the sort.' She paused for a moment and then said: 'He has passed on, I gather.'

'Yes, ma'am, in 1808.'

Mrs Foxcroft nodded thoughtfully and then turned with a smile to the girl beside her. 'May I call you Sophia? Julius, fetch Sophia a chair and put it where I can see her.'

Mr Foxcroft complied, but Sophia was alarmed to find she was expected to sit within a yard of her hostess, where her every inadequacy could all too easily be observed. She sat down, however, and clasped her hands together in her lap.

'Now,' said Mrs Foxcroft, her thoughtful eyes scanning the girl, 'will you tell me something of yourself? Julius, why don't you

101

show Miss Woodeforde some of the house? I'm sure we shall get on famously without you!'

Mr Foxcroft responded with alacrity and by extending an arm to Eliza forced her to acquiesce in a scheme she could not like. Sophia was too nervous; it was too soon to subject her to an inquisition.

'They will have a delightful cose without us, I expect,' Mr Foxcroft said, closing the door quietly. 'Though I dare say you will find a tour of the house quite deadly dull!'

Forgetting her charge momentarily, Eliza glanced at him in surprise. 'Not a bit of it! It's a beautiful old house and I can't wait to see it!'

Mr Foxcroft smiled at her. She reddened a little, conscious of the sudden enthusiasm she had shown, and said, to cover her confusion: 'I love old houses, do not you? I had heard Ingham was fine, but you cannot conceive my envy when I saw it!'

'Envy of Miss Crawley?' he queried, the smile latent.

She turned her frosty gaze upon him. 'Hardly, sir! But of you, for living here! Do you not love it?'

He smiled now in earnest. 'I suppose I do, though I have always lived here, you know, so I suppose I don't appreciate it as I should.'

She sighed. 'You are right of course. How sad that one can never appreciate things until they are lost!'

He gave a startled laugh. 'Surely not

102

everything, Miss Woodeforde!'

She shrugged and smiled. 'Perhaps not. No doubt it is just one of my fanciful ideas!' She glanced about her and said lightly: 'Are these tapestries original? They look very old!'

'They are, don't touch them! They are extraordinarily valuable, or I dare say I should have stripped them down long ago.'

'You don't care for them?'

He shrugged. 'Do you not find them dark? My mother loves them, which is another reason why I haven't removed them, and then too there is my heir to think of, whoever he might be.'

Eliza smiled somewhat sourly, but restrained her impetuous remark.

They had gained a long gallery by this time and Eliza saw it contained portraits of Foxcrofts long dead. 'Your ancestors, Mr Foxcroft?' Eliza said, glancing up at him.

He laughed consciously. 'Yes. Visitors are supposed to be interested in these things, you know, so you must dispense with that bored expression, if you please, and assume one of polite inquiry.'

She obliged, cocking her head and looking at him expectantly. He laughed and drew her hand within his arm. She did not resist and they walked on down the gallery.

'Here, Miss Woodeforde, you can observe the likeness of the earliest known Foxcroft. That is, doubtless there were Foxcrofts before him, but he was the first to have his likeness taken. And a regular thatchgallows he was too, by all accounts.' He glanced at her and laughed. 'Like me, Miss Woodeforde? Don't deny it, I can tell by your expression!'

'So easy to read, Mr Foxcroft?'

'Sometimes, Miss Woodeforde, yes! I own, when you look at me in such a way I can have no doubt of your feelings.'

She turned her face slightly from him and said: 'You are mistaken. I only wish the best for Miss Crawley.'

'I know it. Has she told you of my suggestion?'

She turned her head sharply, her colour rushing up, and then she smiled reluctantly. 'Yes! But it was odious in you to roast me in such a way!'

'Odious, ma'am? Come now, did you not demand it, just a little? Your opinion of me seemed so very bad!'

'Forgive me for that. I do not usually make judgements on other people's recommendations.'

'But you had heard such terrible things about me?' He smiled at her evident confusion. 'They are mostly all true, you know, but as far as Miss Crawley is concerned I have no intentions of forcing her into an unwelcome marriage. I am not, I hope, so barbaric.'

Miss Woodeforde was silent. She could not decide what Mr Foxcroft was, but she must be grateful for what he had done. Finally she said: 'You must think me very bold, sir, but indeed what could I do? Do you not admit that, had I not opened your eyes to the fact of Sophia's uncertainty, you would be very nearly married?'

He smiled. 'I do not deny it, ma'am! Indeed, I was grateful and I cannot imagine what made me blind to what even a fool must have seen!' He shook his head. 'We know each other too little, it is true, but I am hoping that by the end of her stay she may feel differently.'

Eliza had her doubts, but all she said was: 'However did you persuade Sir Lucius to agree to the delay? He seemed determined on an immediate union.'

'My dear Miss Woodeforde, it was simplicity itself! I simply showed him how to achieve what he most wanted.'

'You did? You mean Susan March?'

He nodded. 'You cannot imagine his joy, though he tried to conceal it from me of course!'

She chuckled. 'So that was your idea! I should have guessed, I suppose! Now you tell me I see it has your mark upon it!'

'Has it indeed!' He raised his brows quizzically at her. 'There now! And I thought we had cried truce!'

She laughed up at him. 'Truce, sir? Now, wherever had you such a notion?'

He smiled himself and said: 'Foolish, was it

not! Now, do you not think you had better pay attention? My mother is sure to quiz you about what you have learned!'

'What a fearful thought! Very well, I am now in a learning spirit. Tell me, who is this frightful character whose look you have so exactly?'

They proceeded comfortably down the gallery, observing the features of dead persons for as long as Miss Woodeforde could retain interest. As soon as he sensed her weariness, however, he drew her away, saying with a light smile: 'Come and see our Minstrel's Gallery! Did you notice it from the Hall earlier? It is supposed to be one of the finest examples of the period.'

She stepped forward eagerly and he drew aside a long, very worn curtain that had been suspended at a low archway. A shallow step led them onto the narrow gallery, affording her a magnificent view of the ancient hall with its splendid fire. 'How lucky you were to be born a Foxcroft!' she exclaimed artlessly, stepping forward and leaning over the rail.

She was startled to be dragged roughly back, Mr Foxcroft pulling her so sharply that she fell against the rear wall, striking her head painfully. 'Forgive me!' he cried, staring anxiously into her face. 'I should have warned you. The barrier is quite worm-eaten, I'm afraid. You would have broken your neck.'

She pressed her hand to her temple. The

knock had made her dizzy for a moment, so that she barely heard him speak. She swayed a little and he caught her arm, guiding her back into the picture gallery.

'Sit down,' he said, pulling forward a carved wooden chair. 'It will bear your weight, I promise you.'

She smiled weakly and complied. 'I am quite all right,' she said as he bent over her concernedly. 'Do not distress yourself, it was foolish of me.'

'On the contrary, it was the ✦action of anyone. I cannot imagine how I came to make such a terrible error.'

She shook her head and smiled. 'It is no matter. Shall we go on? I'm sure there is a great deal more to see!'

'Yes, Miss Woodeforde, but I fear it must wait.' He had been consulting his pocket-watch and now said: 'We must return to my mother and Miss Crawley. Do you realize it is past seven? They will be wondering what has become of us, and Armand, my chef, will be tearing his hair in frustration!'

She rose at once and permitted Mr Foxcroft to take her arm.

'Julius!' exclaimed his mother when they entered the drawing-room some minutes later. 'Where have you been? I declare we were quite anxious about you!'

Mr Foxcroft smiled. 'I have been trying, I regret to say, to send Miss Woodeforde crashing to her death.'

Eliza exclaimed and laughed, but Mrs Foxcroft, her expression grave, said severely: 'Julius, what are you talking of? What have you been doing?'

'The Minstrel's Gallery, Mama. Miss Woodeforde's interest was, incredibly, so large that I quite forgot the condition of the barrier. However, I remembered in time to save her, with no greater damage, I trust, than a slight bump on the head.'

'Not even that!' Miss Woodeforde asserted, smiling. 'I own, I was a little startled to be so roughly treated, but I must be very grateful to Mr Foxcroft for his speedy thinking.'

Mrs Foxcroft looked very gravely at her son. All she said, however, was: 'Please ring for Sterne. Dinner is already delayed.'

The dining-chamber in which they presently sat proved worthy of Miss Woodeforde's discerning eye. A fair-sized room, it was panelled throughout, the darkness of the wood counteracted by the many branches Mr Foxcroft had caused to be set about the room. When Miss Woodeforde commented on the unusual quality of the wood she learned that it was Spanish mahogany and had in fact been stripped from the ceremonial apartments of a Spanish man-o'-war, captured by one Edward Foxcroft, whose joy it had been to provide bounty for her Majesty, Queen Elizabeth of course.

'Then it is earlier than the house?' Eliza exclaimed wonderingly.

'Yes, indeed. It belonged in the first Ingham to be erected on this site. Jeremiah Foxcroft despised it, for some reason, and had it torn down. The panelling is all that remains from that house, with the exception of a single arch, left, I fear, for purely romantic reasons. You may see it from your window.'

'I have seen it!' exclaimed Sophia, who had remained silent and abstracted until now. 'Did I not remark, Eliza—oh you were not there! But I remarked to Clara, the maid, how perfectly delightful it was to possess a ruin!'

Mr Foxcroft smiled and turned his attentions to his fiancée for the first time that evening.

His attempts at conversation could not have been called successful. After this unselfconscious declaration Sophia seemed to recollect herself, answering both Mr Foxcroft and his mother in monosyllables. Mrs Foxcroft's questions tended to probe, Eliza noticed, and she inquired about her home and education, but since Sophia was no more communicative than civility required Mrs Foxcroft did not learn very much. Consequently when Mr Foxcroft joined them in the drawing-room she beckoned to Eliza, leaving the happy couple to converse by themselves.

'You cannot conceive, my dear,' Mrs

Foxcroft said as Eliza drew up a chair, 'how pleased I was to learn you would accompany Miss Crawley. The situation, as I understand it, was not a usual one, Miss Crawley having no female companion but yourself since the death of her mother.'

'Yes, ma'am. Sir Lucius's temperament makes him dislike company and, though I say it myself, I cannot but believe the arrangement to have been happier than if she had been consigned to the care of some—unknown relative.'

Mrs Foxcroft smiled slightly. 'My son has told me a little of Miss March.'

'Has he indeed? Then I need not hedge my words, ma'am! Miss March is a most disagreeable woman! Sophia must have been miserable in her care.'

'I make no doubt,' Mrs Foxcroft answered soberly, glancing in Sophia's direction. 'I was pleased to find what a sensible woman has had charge of her education, even though you are still so very young!'

Eliza smiled. 'I am four and twenty, ma'am!'

'Well, well, I dare say it seems a very great age to you, but it is not, believe me!' She cocked her head at Eliza and said: 'Tell me, what became of my old friend, Clarence?'

Eliza sighed. 'He went to India, ma'am. While there he contracted the fever common in those parts and it remained with him even after he returned to England. Gradually it debilitated him until, what with the failure of his expectations, he gave himself up to it. That was six years ago, ma'am.'

'And you still miss him?'

She nodded. 'If you knew him you will know how unconcerned he was, how he never worried about the slightest thing! Sometimes I used to feel almost older than he was, for you must know he had no natural sense! I cannot count the scrapes I was obliged to extricate us from, even as a child!'

Mrs Foxcroft smiled. 'He was considerably younger than I, but I remember so very well how certain he was he would make his fortune by some scheme or other. Did he never do so?'

'Oh yes, a score of times! But he always lost it again, as quickly as he had amassed it! I cannot think of half a dozen times when we had more than the pennies in our pockets. Until the end of course.'

'The end?'

'Papa took a teaching post at a seminary in Tunbridge Wells. He was obliged to learn the Italian tongue rather faster than his pupils, but we contrived, he and I together. That was the first time we had been settled.'

'And how came you to Malham Park?'

'When my father died I didn't feel I could stay any longer and as I was then eighteen I decided my best course was to seek genteel employment.' Her eyes travelled to where Sophia and Mr Foxcroft stood and she smiled slightly.

'Miss Crawley does you credit,' Mrs Foxcroft remarked suddenly. 'My son told me she was unaffected, but I had not expected such complete—artlessness.'

'Had you not?' Miss Woodeforde contemplated her silently for a moment. 'Miss Crawley is one of the kindest, most gentle creatures I have met,' she said suddenly. 'A more generous spirit you could not hope to meet with, I promise you.' Her eyes contemplated them again as they sorted some music on the pianoforte and she saw Mr Foxcroft urge the girl to play. Sophia was blushing and smiling shyly and finally seated herself.

'Miss Woodeforde,' Mrs Foxcroft addressed her suddenly, making her jerk her head. 'Do you dislike the match?'

Eliza was startled and for a moment knew not what to say. 'No, ma'am,' she answered finally, 'and it is not my place to do so. Sir Lucius has given his consent.'

'Nevertheless, Miss Woodeforde, you are uneasy. Please be frank with me. I prefer plain speaking.'

Eliza hesitated. Glancing at the old woman she saw that the faded blue eyes were dagger-sharp and knew it would not do to fence with her hostess. 'Sophia is so young, ma'am,' she answered finally, 'younger even than her years. Your son's proposal was very sudden, she had no time to grow accustomed to it. Her . . . her understanding, although not meagre, is by no means the equal of his. She finds it hard, very often, to comprehend him.' She turned again as the first strains of melody filled the room and for a moment considered them. 'But Mr Foxcroft is very kind with her, I cannot deny it. And then too he has proposed a longer engagement than was originally planned. In short, ma'am, what right have I to dislike something so clearly to my Sophia's benefit?'

'Financially, I assume you to mean,' Mrs Foxcroft concurred dryly. 'Well, I asked for your opinion, so I must be grateful.' She considered a moment and then said: 'She certainly has beauty, Miss Woodeforde, and I see that your tuition on the pianoforte has not gone unrewarded.'

Eliza smiled thinly. 'She was always eager to learn, Mrs Foxcroft, and I have no apprehensions that she will not continue to be so, when married to Mr Foxcroft.'

They exchanged glances of understanding, but the piece was just then finished and they had no time for more. Sophia received the congratulations of the company as she should, but then began pressing Eliza to display her own talent. To this Eliza would not agree. She knew herself to be superior to her pupil and had no desire to offer herself for comparison. She declined the invitation therefore, saying she played but rarely, and then only for her own amusement. It seemed for a moment as though Miss Crawley would persist, but Mr Foxcroft dexterously turned the conversation and the matter was allowed to drop.

'How glad I am we are not far distant!' Sophia remarked as they climbed the stairs later. 'I'm sure I don't know how I shall ever find my way!'

'Of course you will!' Eliza answered bracingly. 'You will be amazed how quickly you will learn and it is such a wonderful house you cannot but love it.'

'Do you really think so?' Sophia said wonderingly. 'Do you not find it dark, Eliza, and sinister? I'm sure I do.'

Eliza smiled. 'Not really, no! But then I always have loved old buildings.'

Sophia shuddered. 'I can't help remembering the terrible accident you almost had today!'

They had gained Sophia's room by this time but Eliza turned round in amazement, her hand on the doorknob. 'What accident? Whatever are you talking of?'

'The Minstrel's Gallery! Surely you have not forgot!'

'Oh. Yes, I admit I had. But then it was not so very dreadful, you know, and Mr Foxcroft saved me before anything happened, so really there was little to concern me!'

Sophia shook her head. 'How calm you are, Eliza, indeed! I'm sure I should have been

114

quite in hysterics over it.'

Eliza shrugged and opened the door. 'How do you like Mrs Foxcroft?' she asked, dropping into a chair. She could not feel a discussion of the trivial incident to be beneficial.

'Very well, I suppose,' Sophia answered diffidently, 'but she is so very proud, isn't she. I'm sure she had me quite in a fidget when you left us alone! However, she was mostly very kind.'

'What did she ask you, Sophy?'

'About Malham and our style of life. I'm afraid she thought we lived very poorly, but what could I say? After here anywhere seems quite insignificant!'

Eliza secretly agreed but she said stoutly: 'What fustian, Sophy! You know you have nothing to blush for in your home or your papa. Mrs Foxcroft knows you have been kept very close and it must please her to learn what your home life has been; and as for Ingham being so large, well, that is surely nothing! Only imagine how large Malham would seem to someone from the village, while to you who have lived there all your life it seems quite natural.'

'So Mr Foxcroft finds Ingham quite natural too?'

'Of course.'

Sophia gave no answer, but Eliza could not feel she was perfectly convinced.

The worries of Miss Crawley were nothing

to those of her fiancé's mother. Mrs Foxcroft, far from being eased by her introduction to the girl, had been greatly disturbed, and not only by her extreme youthfulness and innocence. She had noticed the effort made by her son to entertain the young woman and wondered how long it would be before the enthusiasm he presently felt dwindled and died. She could not think it would be long. Already she had seen his eye upon Miss Woodeforde and although she could not feel anything would transpire of an encounter with a governess she yet wondered how long it would be before her son sought amusements of quite a different order. She kept her fears to herself, however, merely saying to her son when he asked that she found Miss Crawley a very prettily behaved young woman, but that she would know better when she dropped her extreme reserve.

'You must understand,' her son explained carefully, 'how delicately she has been reared. She has barely left her home until recently and then has attended the balls in Bath under the strict chaperonage of Lady Winterton. But I am sure, when she feels more at home, you will find her quite as charming as I do.'

'I'm sure I will,' was his mama's reply. But she went to bed in some anxiety and shortly grew convinced that only the appearance on the scene of a *femme fatale* could cure her son of his madness.

116

CHAPTER SIX

The following morning the two young ladies found themselves left to their own devices. Since neither had slept well they descended early to breakfast, but Mr Foxcroft had been in advance of them and was now riding his estates with his steward. As Mrs Foxcroft invariably remained in her chamber until after noon they were able to wander as they liked, something neither felt inclined to regret. Sophia's interest in the house being minimal, they walked in the grounds and consequently were in an excellent position to observe the arrival of an antiquated travelling chariot, from which presently emerged two lively black spaniels, and a tall person, swathed in an old-fashioned evening-cloak and wearing a felt hat with a long, upstanding feather.

'What an extraordinary-looking gentleman!' Sophia exclaimed, as the person turned to issue instructions to the coachman. 'Only see how worn his cloak is, and he is wearing it in the day, Eliza!'

'So he is,' Eliza concurred, wondering herself who this oddity could be. Just then the figure turned suddenly and she had an impression of piercing grey eyes and sharp nose before they found themselves addressed in strident tones.

'You, whoever you are, kindly desist! There is nothing I abominate more than being talked about behind my back!' She stared intently at them for a moment longer and then said sharply: 'Be so good as to approach. I should like to see who I am addressing.'

Sophia hesitated, but Eliza, her fancy caught, stepped forward at once and stretched out her hand. 'Good-morning! I am Eliza Woodeforde and this is Miss Crawley. We are guests here also and I'm afraid I do not know where Mr Foxcroft is.'

'It is not of the least consequence,' the lady answered briskly. 'I am expected, so doubtless some flunkey will show me to my chamber. However, I shall be downstairs directly and should be grateful if you would await my return. No doubt there is a drawing-room of some description in this rambling monstrosity!'

'Yes, of course, but—'

'Please, I have had a tiresome morning! Would you be so kind as to exercise my animals? I shall not be above fifteen minutes.'

Eliza would have protested but the creature turned on her heels as she spoke, leaving the two dogs to frisk about the young woman as if they had understood what their mistress had said.

'Whatever shall we do?' exclaimed Sophia, contemplating the animals in dismay. 'Do you think they are dangerous?'

'Hardly!' Eliza returned, laughing. 'And

118

what should we do, pray, but what we are bid?'

Sophia laughed, but said: 'Who do you suppose she is? I declare I was never more surprised than when she spoke to us, were you?'

'It was unexpected, yes!' Eliza agreed, stooping down to fondle the animals that scampered about her. 'I dare say she is some relation, though she clearly has not been here before or she would have known where the drawing-room was.'

'Yes,' agreed Sophia pensively. 'How very odd!'

However this was, when they later made their way to the blue drawing-room, the dogs having been consigned to the care of a young and grinning footman, the lady had arrived in advance of them and was now pacing the room, smoking, Eliza noticed with amusement, a cheroot. Since the room was already smoke-filled she had clearly been there some little time, which impression she at once confirmed by saying briskly: 'At last! What dawdlers you both are! Where are my children?'

Sophia stared, but Eliza, her calm unruffled, replied: 'With one of the footmen, ma'am. He is walking with them in the park.'

'Humph.' She walked with long mannish strides to the window and peered out through its leaded panes. The black coat and hat had been removed and the woman now stood revealed in a gown of rusty black merino, cut with a very full skirt for maximum freedom of movement. It was shapeless and lacking in style, but the wearer herself amply made up for any deficiency of colour. She stared for some moments without comment and then turned her searing gaze upon themselves. 'So you are Sophia!' she remarked, moving swiftly to Miss Crawley and catching her chin. 'I suppose you have something of your mother, though her hair was corn, not flaxen. So insipid!' She stared a moment longer and then released her. 'Well, girl, tell me about yourself. I have come far enough, the Lord knows!' She drew on her cheroot and blew smoke upwards where it swirled about the decorated ceiling.

Eliza smiled. 'Forgive us, ma'am, but you have the advantage of us!'

'I do?' The lady turned steeled eyes upon Eliza. 'You, of all females, should know who I am! You have even impersonated me!'

'Impers—Then you must be Miss Stanley!' Realization and recollection came simultaneously. Flushing, she said stiffly: 'Mr Foxcroft told you of me, I collect. I hate to think what your opinion must be!'

The gaze did not soften, but Miss Stanley said: 'You were foolhardy, were you not, miss! However, I like a girl with pluck and you have that aplenty, it seems to me!'

Eliza reddened uncomfortably, but said: 'If you knew my reasons, ma'am—!'

'I know 'em well enough,' Miss Stanley dryly

responded. 'Though I'm danged if I can see how you thought such a crack-brained scheme could put the matter to rights! He must have bubbled you in the end, and then what should you do but return by weeping cross?'

Eliza shook her head. 'At the time there seemed no other way!'

Miss Stanley grunted. 'A straightforward supplication naturally did not suggest itself!'

'No, for I thought—in short, Miss Stanley, I thought Mr Foxcroft so puffed up in his own esteem that only the threat of disinheritance would make him withdraw!'

'Fair and far out, ain't you!' she chuckled and sat down in a deep armchair. 'Told him that meself. Never did the least particle of good. If you ask my opinion, his mind's set on this match. Heart too, I shouldn't wonder.' She contemplated Sophia a moment and then said sharply: 'Well, miss, what have you to say for yourself? You're mighty close for someone with such a paramount interest!'

Sophia started and flushed. 'Me, ma'am?'

'Yes, you! Or are you such a pea-goose you don't realise we've been speaking of your affairs this last half-hour!'

'Of course! That is, yes! But now Mr Foxcroft has proposed a longer engagement it doesn't signify so greatly, does it? Of course I'm very grateful to you for your concern,' she added hurriedly.

'Heaven save me!' exclaimed Miss Stanley,

121

rising and walking swiftly about the room. 'I can't think much of your abilities, Miss Whoever-you-are, if your training has produced such muddle-headed thinking in my niece!' She turned sharply to Sophia and said: 'You don't think to marry him at the last, then, miss? You intend crying off?'

'No! That is—I don't know!'

She turned huge eyes to Eliza for aid, but Miss Stanley, seeing this, said curtly: 'It's no use looking to your governess for assistance either! If you don't like the match say so! This skimble-skamble reasoning ain't no particle of use with me!'

Sophia flushed darkly and stammered: 'Truly, I don't know! I thought—I thought perhaps if I knew him better—' She stopped and looked desperately from one to the other.

'Humph. You thought if you came to know him better you might not feel so badly about it, eh? But what if you did? What then?'

'Well, I suppose—I suppose I would tell him!' She finished on a rush.

'When you had not the courage before? Moonshine!' She glared so hard at Sophia that the girl, confused and bewildered, burst into tears.

'Miss Stanley, I must ask you to desist! Miss Crawley is not used to your style of questioning!'

'Not used!' The old woman watched while Eliza led Sophia to a seat and then said gruffly: 'I'll wager her Papa has a rough tongue with him, has he not? She should be used to it!'

'Her Papa loves her sincerely!' Eliza answered roundly. 'His rough ways may seem a little strange at first, but not to Sophia, who has known him all her life! You, ma'am, she has not! She has but this instant made your acquaintance, you having been content to remain a recluse all her life!'

Miss Stanley's face was expressionless. She stared in turn at Eliza and the sniffing Sophia and then, to Miss Woodeforde's consternation, gave a sharp, barking laugh. 'Well said, miss, a palpable hit; but you cannot but admit it to be a senseless scheme! If she has no notion of marrying the fellow she should tell him to his head, now!'

Eliza shook her head. 'Sir Lucius is so anxious for the match, ma'am, she does not wish to disappoint him!'

'Hornswoggle!' exclaimed Miss Stanley.

'No, ma'am, not if you were to understand the situation.'

Miss Stanley was silent. After a few minutes Sophia managed to calm herself, but she felt unable to continue the conversation and left the room.

'My recollection,' Miss Stanley remarked, 'is generally excellent. Surely my brother-in-law is as selfish and nipfarthing as I have always imagined him?'

'Yes, ma'am, I dare say. However, do not underestimate Miss Crawley's affection! Indeed she feels his own to be such that, centred even as it is upon self-interest, she cannot bear to see him disappointed. And I must own, I cannot but believe that, if he thought the match truly evil, he could not countenance it.'

'But you, Miss Woodeforde, have taken it upon yourself to disapprove. Presumption, is it not, in a mere governess?'

Eliza raised her chin. 'A governess I might be, ma'am, but I have a sincere affection for Miss Crawley! In fact she is the only family I should ever care to claim. Can you truly consider happiness in store for these persons?'

Miss Stanley was silent. Her humour tempted her to argue in the face of anything, but here, she saw, was a young woman whose clear head should not lightly be dismissed. 'No, Miss Woodeforde, I cannot.'

'Then you will support me, with Sir Lucius?'

'I cannot, Miss Woodeforde. I owe something to Mr Foxcroft, after all.'

Eliza stared. 'What, in heaven's name?'

Miss Stanley smiled sourly. 'He has invited me, you should remember. Has it not occurred to you that we might be bosom-bows?'

It had not and Eliza's countenance showed plainly the dismay he felt. In her attempts to win the assistance of this strangely formidable female she had quite overlooked the fact that

Miss Stanley had arrived, quite unlooked for, at Ingham, a guest of Julius Foxcroft.

But a surprise remained in store for them all and Jemima Stanley proved to be not the only visitor that day to Ingham. Mr Foxcroft, returning from his day's outing, was not a little concerned to see a carriage, laden with the baggage for a month's residence, stationary before his home and the short plump form of his sister just then being conducted inside. Frowning in irritation he spurred up his mount, arriving in his stables just as the carriage was brought round. Watching ill-temperedly as the sweating beasts were led away, he demanded of the coachman how many persons he had conducted thither.

The fellow touched his forelock in respect but his reply struck doom to Mr Foxcroft's soul. 'Three, sir. My lady, the dowager, and her daughter and Mr Carleton Davenham.'

Mr Foxcroft groaned. That his sister should bring Mary he had expected, and even smiled a little when he thought of the impishness of his young niece. His sister's nephew, however, the son of the present Lord Ludlow, made him raise his eyes to heaven and it did not take a great deal of thought to see where his sister's hopes lay. At twenty-three Carleton Davenham embodied all the perfections of a witless Apollo. His clear blue eyes gazed with simple faith upon the evils of the world so that his father, a man of no common intellect, had been heard to murmur in his cups that the child must have been a changeling. Certainly Carleton bore no resemblence to any of the Davenhams; but when one looked upon the visage of the present Lady Ludlow one knew the gentleman's claims to be groundless. Angelically fair, Lady Ludlow had the intelligence, as her husband often told her, of a flea. With his mother's looks and temperament Carleton was ill-fitted, in his father's eyes, to assume the position that would one day necessarily be his, yet all his attempts to inculcate the inadequate brain with some education had failed. Carleton remained, as ever, handsome and gentle, a favourite with the ladies for his countenance and address, scorned by the gentlemen for his inability to control a curricle and four, or shoot the pips from a playing-card at twenty paces. It took very little thought to lay bare his sister's schemes and Mr Foxcroft's lip curled as he strode towards the house, tapping his crop impatiently against his boot.

He found his sister already closeted in the chamber of her youth. A business-like 'Come in' came in response to his peremptory knock and he entered to discover his sister supervising the disposal of her belongings.

'Ah, Julius! How good of you to come as soon as I asked for you! Such a stupid thing, no doubt an oversight by your housekeeper, but I'm sure you will have it attended to at

126

once.'

'I will, Antonia?' responded her brother in tones far from conciliatory.

'Now, Julius,' reproved his sister, directing with one finger the laying out of an evening-dress, 'I hope you are not in one of your disobliging tempers! You must know how it is! There is no chamber prepared for poor Carleton and the one my dearest Mary uses is already occupied! How can this be, Julius, when I wrote to you so particularly of our visit?'

'You did?'

Mr Foxcroft's tone was dry and bored, but his sister barely noticed, for just then her attention and indignation was drawn upon another. 'Not *there,* girl! Only see how you have creased the sleeve! Really, I'm sure I shall never know why Miss Crimpton left me in such a thoughtless way! These town girls, you know, Julius, have not the slightest notion of industry! No, girl, that will not do at all. You shall have to press it.' She sighed heavily and turned her gaze upon her brother. 'The fact that the sheets on my bed are damp, Julius, I may perhaps excuse, and a hot brick laid now between them will surely remedy it. But to give your own niece's room to another, well—! It is not a kindness, that is all I can say. Whatever was she to think, pray, when she found her chamber so occupied?'

'I was not aware, Antonia, that she could lay

claim to any chamber in my home.'

'Oh well, as to that—but that's neither here nor there. I'm sure I have no wish to quarrel with you and if the woman cannot be ousted then Mary must content herself with somewhere else. Only do not forget, Julius! Indeed it never ceases to amaze me how extraordinarily forgetful you are.'

'I must be indeed,' he responded grimly, 'since I have no recollection at all of having invited you.'

His sister laughed somewhat consciously. 'What did I tell you! However, I'll not come to cuffs with you over such a trifling thing, since I'm sure it is soon remedied.'

'Certainly. You may tell your maid not to dispose of any more of your possessions.'

The control the dowager had exercised threatened to snap. 'Julius, you are monstrous unkind, I declare! We shall see what Mama has to say of it when she hears!'

'She does not know?' Mr Foxcroft said wonderingly. 'Indeed I had almost suspected you were about to say she had invited you.'

Since it had been in her mind to say just this Lady Ludlow could think of no suitable retort, so she contented herself with sniffing and saying irritably: 'I'm sure I never knew a more disagreeable brother! Anyone would think you were not pleased to see me!'

'How can I be, Antonia, when we never meet without coming to blows?'

128

'Well, I'm sure it is not my fault if we do! However,' she said, forcing a smile to her lips, 'I have not come here to argue. In fact if I did not know you better I should think you had provoked me on purpose, since you are perfectly well aware you shall not send me away.'

Mr Foxcroft was silent. His inclination was to summon his sister's carriage without delay and follow the advice he had once given to Sir Lucius Crawley, but his mother was at Ingham. Although Antonia bore little real affection for her remaining parent she yet claimed a great deal and Mr Foxcroft knew that a disagreement of such a magnitude between them could only be productive of great distress for his mother. In fact his sister had relied upon this when she had come. She was regarding him now with considerable triumph in her pale blue eyes and for a moment Mr Foxcroft felt possessed of some quite murderous inclinations. He managed to repress these, however, and asked, with a curl to his lips, where the young people just then were.

'Oh, I'm sure I don't know,' his sister responded carelessly. 'There were some dogs, or some such thing, in the shrubbery. Well, you know how ridiculous Carleton is about dogs! No sooner did he see them than he was gone and I dare say it will be quite dinner-time before we see him again. And as for Mary, well, she does just as she pleases! I'm sure I don't know why I am so afflicted! Not but what she's a delight to me of course,' she added hastily, seeing the derision re-enter her brother's scornful eyes.

He rose now and took his leave, but at the door he turned to say: 'Do not forget early dinner, Antonia! We keep country hours at Ingham and Mama dislikes to be kept waiting.'

Considerably irritated he strode from the room, closing the door with some force. A heavy frown drawing his black brows together across his nose he descended the stairs looking like a thundercloud, causing a junior footman to remark somewhat later that something had occurred to make the master as surly as a butcher's dog, and impertinently warn Sterne to take care when waiting on his master that evening.

By the time he reached the shrubbery, however, Mr Foxcroft's ill-temper had somewhat abated and he was able to greet Mr Davenham with something like civility. The fact that Mary had joined her cousin outside might have had much to do with this, for although Mr Foxcroft found Carleton's slow wits and gentle nature not to his taste he had a considerable affection for his spirited niece and consequently bit back the cutting words.

'I say, sir!' exclaimed Carleton by way of greeting. 'See what fine beasts! This good fellow says they belong to a Miss Stanley, or some such person.'

Absently Mr Foxcroft bent to fondle a smooth black head, indicating to the hovering footman to leave them alone, but Mary said, with a mischievous smile: 'I'll warrant you did not think to see us so soon, Uncle Julius!'

He smiled back. 'Minx! You must know I did not! What is your mama about, I wonder?'

'Do you? Really, Uncle, I had thought you owned more sense!'

He chuckled, but the presence of the young man prevented his retort and he said instead: 'How do you do, Carleton. It is some time, I think, since we saw you at Ingham.'

'Lord, yes! And I was never more surprised, I can tell you, than when Aunt Antonia invited me! But she said she feared highwaymen and needed escorting, so what could I do indeed?'

'I don't know what imaginable use you'd have been though,' Mary told him frankly, slipping an arm into one each of her cousin's and uncle's. 'You do not know which end of a pistol to hold, I believe!'

Carleton grinned good-humouredly. 'She's in the right of it, sir!' he admitted with an honest air. 'Though I don't hold with killing, as you know.' He jerked his arm away from Mary as he spoke and received the stick he had previously thrown for one of the dogs. 'Good boy! What capital animals, sir, are they not? I wonder who Miss Stanley can be?'

'An aunt of Miss Crawley,' Mr Foxcroft

responded somewhat dryly, watching as Carleton caught the stick from the dog again and hurled it away.

'Then we'll meet her at dinner,' Mary remarked, glancing up at her tall uncle. 'And shall I meet Miss Crawley too?'

Mr Foxcroft nodded. 'Most certainly. Indeed it seems we are quite a party. I had better speak with Armand or we shall find ourselves without any dinner.' They walked on a little way, while Carleton, occupied as he was with the dogs, gradually became left behind.

'Well, Uncle Julius,' cried Mary, hanging on his arm and grinning up at him, 'are you pleased to see us all? I knew it would be a surprise for you, so I said I'd come too, though Mama was most urgent with me to remain with Jane! But how could I miss such fun, Uncle, as there's sure to be?'

'So you enjoy a good brangle, do you? Well, it seems to me as though we'll be at each other's throats before the evening's out, so you'll have more than your share of enjoyment.'

'So I thought! But I wonder you did not expect Mama to do something of the sort! She's as mad as fire with you, you should know.'

'I do know,' he responded dryly, 'though what business it is of hers I fail to conceive.'

'Oh, none at all! That's what makes it all the more diverting.'

Mr Foxcroft looked down at her amusedly. 'You know, miss, that's a very disloyal way of speaking of your mother. I ought not to allow it.'

'But you do, don't you, because you agree with me.' Her smile faded and she grew thoughtful. 'In truth, I wish Mama would not fly so into the boughs. I've tried to tell her I really don't mind about Ingham, but it won't fadge. She just doesn't listen to me, you see, so what can I do? She feels us such a trial to her and, I must own, when I see myself in the mirror I wonder if I will ever take! Do you know, she was used to think she could make a match for me with Carleton, but can you imagine it, Uncle! I mean, not that he isn't very good-natured, I know, but, have you ever wondered if he had—well—a screw loose?'

Mr Foxcroft smiled. 'Mary, you must learn to curb your tongue! That manner of speaking is all very well to me, but what would your Mama think, or your Grandmama, if she were to hear you?'

'She wouldn't,' Mary answered frankly. 'I only speak this way to you, so don't stop me, please, because I feel constricted enough as it is!'

'Very well,' he responded obligingly, squeezing her hand slightly, 'but I think you might find a kindred spirit here tonight.'

'Miss Crawley, you mean?'

He shook his head. 'No, Miss Eliza

133

Woodeforde, the governess-companion.'

'Oh.' For a moment Mary was silent and when she spoke again it was on the exigencies of their journey.

Within the confines of her own room Sophia had been giving vent to the pent-up emotions of several weeks. Eliza, entering a little later, was disturbed to find her so distressed, but said in a bracing tone: 'Really, Sophia, what is it that you are so upset? I'm sure crying never did the least particle of good to anyone!'

Sophia gave her a reproachful glance, but made an effort to stop and after a moment dried her face. 'How could I be so stupid?' she exclaimed, sniffing angrily into her handkerchief. 'Until my aunt told me I had not truly realized how it was.'

Eliza frowned. 'Whatever do you mean? What did she make you realize?'

'That I should have to marry Mr Foxcroft in the end!' she wailed, burying her nose once more in her handkerchief.

'But Sophy—I thought—Dearest, I do not understand you!'

'I know,' Sophia answered, her voice muffled. 'And when I think of it I do not understand myself.' She stood up and stared in a blind way about her before grasping her discarded shawl. 'I think I shall walk a little, Eliza. Do you mind? I'm so confused I hardly know what I am about!'

Eliza did not answer. She watched silently

134

as Sophia flung her wrap inexpertly about her shoulders and virtually ran from the room.

Hurrying down the stairs, Sophia almost fell. She caught her boot in the flounce of her new muslin gown and stumbled and only her frantic clasping of the banister saved her from being cast to the bottom. She stared confusedly at the footman who had started towards her and then began fumbling with the ancient iron handles of the front door. When the footman quietly turned them for her she started in surprise, barely murmuring her thanks as she stumbled into the Spring sunshine. Outside and alone she grew calmer, hurrying across the damp grass towards the shrubbery with very little regard for the welfare of her gown which trailed unheeded in the dirt. Breathing deeply as Miss Woodeforde had taught her, she began to think more sensibly about her predicament. There was no denying but that her new-found aunt had greatly disturbed her. A solitary tear coursed its way unnoticed down her cheek and hung suspended while she looked confusedly about her. She had wandered into a denser part of the shrubbery without realizing and now could see nothing but the bushes and small trees of which it was composed. Ahead of her, however, was a rustic seat, cut from a log of wood and set into a small clearing. Her wrap trailing from one shoulder she sat down and began pulling at the dark glossy leaves of a laurel. How long she sat she knew not, but a chill wind had just reminded her about her lost wrap when a shaggy black dog, his coat sodden, presented himself before her and shook himself violently. Sophia screamed. The animal, one of Miss Stanley's spaniels, misinterpreted her sudden leap to her feet. Snapping up a dead branch he gambolled about, impeding her attempts to get away. She cried again and stepped backwards, but unfortunately her way was blocked by the spiky twigs of a leafless shrub. Tears streaming down already stained cheeks, she sobbed helplessly until a figure appeared as from nowhere and delivered the beast a sharp reproof about the rump. The spaniel gazed with reproachful eyes upon his former friend and slunk away to chew his stick in private. Finally Carleton turned to look at the damsel he had rescued. Sophia herself could see very little, her eyes being completely water-logged, but she was vaguely aware of the open-mouthed stare with which the gentleman favoured her. Even with her face tear-stained and half-concealed by her handkerchief she looked an angel and, when she had managed to wipe her eyes sufficiently to see, she realized that Carleton himself was far from unheroic in appearance. The fact that he embodied all her preconceived notions of a hero and indeed looked almost exactly how she had imagined Angelina's Sir Percival accounted largely for the nervous smile she

136

now afforded him and the miraculous cessation of her tears. And now Carleton was recollecting his manners. He shut his mouth and said, by way of introducing himself: 'Stupid beast, should have known better! Carleton Davenham, miss!'

Shyly Sophia curtseyed to his bow. 'How—how do you do! Thank you for helping me! I'm sure he meant no harm, but they frighten one so, particularly when they bound about in that terrible way!'

'Of course!' exclaimed Carleton, forgetting his usual scorn for such weakness. 'It must have been quite distressing!' He smiled inanely at her for a moment and then said suddenly: 'Are you a guest? I mean, can I escort you back to the house?'

Sophia nodded shyly and took his proffered arm, but was forced to relinquish it again when her maltreated shawl fell to the ground. Carleton's efforts to place it expeditiously were not very successful, but Sophia seemed not to mind and they finally turned and headed towards the house, the two dogs trotting peaceably at a respectable distance.

'I say!' exclaimed Carleton, grinning suddenly. 'This above all things great! I mean,' he went on, blushing, 'I had no notion there was to be anyone but ourselves here—my aunt and cousin, that is.'

'Your aunt?' Sophia queried, risking one quick glance at his handsome profile.

'Lord, yes! Aunt Antonia! She and Uncle Julius aren't wondrous great, I suspect—at least, no one's ever told me so, but sometimes it almost seems to me—however, that's neither here nor there!' he added hurriedly, flushing darkly.

'Then Mr Foxcroft is your uncle!' exclaimed Sophia, unaware of Carleton's social blunder.

'Oh yes! That is, not really, at least, Aunt Antonia's husband, my Uncle Bertram, was my father's brother. If you can solve it you've a better head than I, for I've no brain for such reckonings!'

'Neither have I. And it is so *odious* to have people always staring at one as if one had a screw loose! Even Eliza, not but what she's the dearest creature, of course-sometimes calls me "a delightful noddle-cock", which might be very well for someone else, but not for oneself!' she finished hurriedly, flushing at these artless disclosures to a stranger.

But Carleton seemed delighted. 'That's it exactly!' he exclaimed, turning to her with a radiant expression. 'Sometimes I even think Uncle Julius finds me a bit of a bore, for he calls me a witless noodle; and though it's only funning I wonder occasionally if he really means it!'

'He's so dreadfully clever, isn't he,' Sophia remarked, her nervous smile replaced by an expression of deep gloom.

Carleton nodded gravely. 'Lord, yes! I

138

declare I hardly ever understand two words he puts together! But my cousin Mary is just the same, you know, though she's a great girl! You'll like her, for she's always straight with one.'

They had gained the house by this time and Carleton, signalling surreptitiously to a footman, indicated by a series of nods and gestures that he wished to consign the dogs to his care. Sophia turned and smiled at her rescuer as they passed through the door, intending to return to her chamber, but a figure was just then descending the stairs towards them and Carleton found himself hailed in reproving tones.

'Carleton! Where have you been? I declare I've been searching for you this half-hour!' It was Lady Ludlow. Sophia, glancing up, saw a woman of full proportions descending the stairs towards them and had the impression of irritation and expensive perfume before the coldly calculating blue eyes were turned upon her. Then the lady smiled. 'You have made the acquaintance of Miss Crawley already, I see, Carleton! Then you shall be able to introduce us, shall you not! I am Lady Ludlow,' she continued without hesitation. 'How do you do! I am so charmed to meet you, my dear, you cannot conceive! Ever since Julius told me of his fascinating romance I have been quite in a fidget over it! Carleton, you may give me your arm. I am looking for my brother, my dear, and feel sure you can take me directly to him!'

If this speech was calculated to set Sophia at her ease it failed miserably. She stared in bewilderment as the older woman took her arm in a companionable way and guided her down the length of the hall.

'And how do you like Ingham, Miss Crawley? Or shall I call you Sophia? Yes, I shall, for we shall be sisters, after all, shall we not, when you and Julius are married!'

Carleton Davenham was walking with his mouth open. Although indeed he rarely paid much attention to his aunt, for even to his ears her talk was just fustian, her last words had served to strike him like a blow from above and he now stared at Sophia in mingled horror and dismay.

'I'm sure I was almost sorry to be married,' Lady Ludlow was saying smoothly, 'when it meant leaving this lovely house. Although, of course, Mandrath is wonderful, so I could not repine for very long, could I! And now, do you know, it will all be Carleton's one day?'

'Ingham will be Carleton's one day?' Sophia said, staring in a bewildered way at Lady Ludlow.

She gave a shallow laugh. 'Gracious me, no! I mean Mandrath, of course! And to speak the truth I think it is quite as grand as Ingham, do not you, Carleton?'

He shook his head unexpectedly. 'No, Aunt, for it ain't *ancient*, like Ingham, nor it hasn't got miles of corridor that make you lose your way as soon as blink! But it's comfortable, and pleasant too.'

'Lord, Carleton!' laughed Lady Ludlow, darting a dagger-glance at her nephew. 'Miss Crawley will think you live in a hovel if you talk such flummery!'

'No she won't,' Carleton replied, an obstinate look about his face. 'She understands very well, I dare say, exactly what I mean.'

'Oh yes!' Sophia cried, smiling up at him. 'For I live in just such a place myself! It's not very grand, or even very beautiful, I suppose, but it is my home and I like it!'

'You see!' Carleton exclaimed jubilantly. 'I knew she'd understand what I meant!'

Lady Ludlow smiled and forbore to argue.

CHAPTER SEVEN

Afterwards Eliza was to find it hard to place the events of the next few days in any reasonable order. With the house full of guests there was rarely a dull moment and if these moments were not always happy it was doubtless because those concerned were so ill-fit to be companions. Whatever Lady Ludlow's plans might have been she certainly had not foreseen the presence of an attractive, albeit penniless, young person of the female gender,

141

but it had taken a very little consideration to discount any danger from that quarter. That her brother's engagement might be terminated, simply that another might be formed, was too ludicrous even to be contemplated. The girl, though not without breeding, was dowerless and a governess besides. Miss Jemima Stanley had presented problems to Lady Ludlow's scheming, however. From the first this strange female had quite mystified the good dowager and the discovery that she apparently held the whole company, with the exception perhaps of her host, in contempt did little for Lady Ludlow's peace of mind. The woman seemed content to take a backward part, however, and with that Lady Ludlow was forced to be satisfied. She was watching the progress of Carleton's infatuation with a considerable degree of pleasure. That everyone else must have observed it likewise could not be avoided, but she did wish that her daughter had not been quite so tiresome about it all. For Mary had made it plain from the first that she did not approve of her mother's actions. All Lady Ludlow's schemes to push the two young people together went awry and usually because Mary obstinately refused to leave them alone, even for so much as a moment. And, when Mary was not there, then the governess creature almost certainly was, until Lady Ludlow felt quite in sympathy with poor Carleton's despairing, hopeless features.

Eliza herself attached little importance to the infatuation. Recognising in the young man all the signs of a first love, she discounted it as such, never for a moment wondering whether Sophia might be susceptible. For indeed where Sophia was concerned Eliza had other worries. The girl seemed out of sorts, it had to be admitted. The youthful bloom that made her countenance so particularly pleasing had vanished and she ate little, so that her cheeks sank in and her eyes looked too large for her face. At first Eliza had hoped it to be a passing cold, but after two days this seemed far from the case and when Sophia finally professed herself too ill to get up Miss Woodeforde decided the doctor had to be sent for.

He came, an elderly, gruff man, who had a very poor opinion of wandering about gardens without wraps in February, as Sophia huskily admitted she had done.

But he felt her pulse and her forehead and after a few minutes more drew Eliza aside to say quietly: 'Tell me, does she often contract infections of this sort?'

Eliza shook her head. Sophia, on the whole, was very hale, although, to be sure, when she did fall ill it was usually with unprecedented intensity.

Dr Glover nodded. 'It's the influenza, right enough,' he said, glancing round as the sound of gentle sobbing came from the bed, 'but she seems sadly pulled. Burning the candle at both ends I make no doubt!'

'No, but there has been some—emotional distress.'

'Ah!' Dr Glover frowned severely at her, his eyebrows jutting heavily over his grey eyes. 'Well, keep her quiet and don't be surprised if her fever mounts. I'll give you some powders, but be certain she takes them.' He turned to go, but in the doorway hesitated and said gruffly: 'I gather Lady Ludlow is here.'

Eliza nodded. 'Yes, together with her daughter and nephew.'

He grunted. 'Keep her from the room, if you please. She's doubtless very well in her way, but a more depressing female I never met! She'll convince Miss Crawley she has scarlet fever or the smallpox, I shouldn't wonder; and in her weakened state—' He shook his head and stared hard at Eliza out of kindly grey eyes.

'Her weakened state?' Eliza echoed, closing the door rather hurriedly behind her. 'You do not anticipate any danger, surely!'

They were moving down the passage by this time but Dr Glover stopped and gently rubbed his chin. 'With attention no. But she is not strong, Miss, despite appearances to the contrary. A chance draught or a shock, you understand, would be most prejudicial, I fear.'

'I see,' Eliza said, though she did not. 'What about the other guests? Should they leave?'

Dr Glover shrugged. 'My dear Miss

144

Woodeforde, it is a matter for themselves to decide. There is always a risk of infection, naturally, but in, say, a strong healthy man a matter of days will see it right.'

'And in Sophy's case?'

'Ah.' Dr Glover stared dolefully over her head. 'A fortnight perhaps.' His eyes dropped to her face and he said gruffly: 'I'll call again in a day or two, but don't hesitate to send for me should anything—well good-day to you, Miss Woodeforde. I'll find my own way.' And he left her, apparently unaware of the highly alarming picture he had painted.

Eliza returned in some haste to the sick-room, but Sophia had dropped into an uneasy slumber. A maid was in attendance, a short, round, country girl, but with the bright eyes of intelligence and sense. She glanced smilingly up at Eliza as the young woman dropped into a chair and then returned to her contemplation of Sophia's face. Eliza herself was in a brown study. The alarm she had first felt on Dr Glover's words was beginning to fade; she began to suspect him of stating the worst, when with proper care and attention—She sighed and rose.

'Clara, ring for me, won't you, should there be any change?' All idea of breakfast had deserted her, but she remembered her invited state and moved reluctantly towards the breakfast-room. Mercifully it was empty, but she had been there barely a minute before the door opened and a distraught Carleton burst into her presence, his cherubic blue eyes dark and anxious.

'Miss Woodeforde!' he exclaimed, striding across valuable carpets regardless of his muddied top-boots. 'Is it really true?'

Eliza eyed him. 'Till I know what you speak of, sir, how can I answer?' she replied, somewhat prosaically, for she had, as yet, no love for this young man. 'Sit down and have some coffee. It's tolerably warm.'

He stared at her, her words apparently unintelligible to him, but after a moment he appeared to recollect himself and dragged out a chair.

'Your pardon,' he muttered in an indistinct way, growing suddenly very red. 'I had heard Miss Crawley was ill and Aunt Antonia, Lady Ludlow, said that scarlet fever—'

Eliza choked back a laugh. 'What nonsense!' she told him roundly. 'It is no more than influenza and I dare say Miss Crawley will be much more the thing in a day or two.' She smiled suddenly, for indeed Carleton looked amazingly crestfallen, and she recollected that if he had fallen in love it was hardly his fault. 'I'm sure there is nothing to fear,' she told him in a kinder tone. 'Of course Dr Glover said she must be cosseted a little and protected from draughts and so on, but that in a week or two—'

'A week or two!' Carleton exclaimed,

jumping up with such violence that his chair crashed over. 'Why, that is forever!'

'Gracious, Carleton, what fustian you talk sometimes!' It was Mary, her grey eyes astute yet cautious in her small, pixie face. 'Miss Woodeforde, good-morning! I was so sorry to hear of poor Miss Crawley's illness! Though I dare say it is not so very bad, despite Carleton's theatricals and Mama's exaggerations!'

'No, Miss Davenham, but she will be in a poor way for several days, I fear.'

'I see.' Mary paused and her glance calmly took in Carleton's muddied boots and shamefully disarranged cravat. 'Really, Carleton, have you seen what a figure you cut? I dare say Miss Woodeforde thinks you quite demented, raving in such a manner! Thank goodness neither Mama nor Uncle Julius can see you!'

Mr Davenham grinned sheepishly and ran a hand through thick, disordered locks. 'Forgive me,' he muttered, blushing deeply. He moved awkwardly to the door, eyeing them alternately and then made a hurried dash and grab for the handle and disappeared.

'Poor Carleton!' Mary sighed, drawing up a chair. 'Do you mind if I sit down? He gets so confused, you know, although he really is quite a pet. Uncle Julius says he has a maggot in his top-loft, but I think he is just . . . terribly disorganised!'

Eliza smiled perfunctorily. 'I dare say,

though I could wish he would not make such a cake of himself over Miss Crawley!'

'No,' agreed Mary thoughtfully, 'but it is just like him, you know. Probably tomorrow he will have found something quite different to divert him!' She smiled. 'Oh yes! In many ways he is just like a child and then in others he is so—oh, infuriatingly stubborn!'

'Well, I only hope you may be right!' Eliza responded with some feeling.

However this was, Carleton spent the day mooning about the house and gardens, serving to exasperate virtually everyone he came into contact with. Even Lady Ludlow began to wonder why she had ever invited him and it was only the recollection that it was all on Mary's account that reconciled her at all. She immediately banished the burgeoning plan of removing herself, Mary and Carleton to London. She contented herself with avoiding Mr Davenham whenever she could, but since he seemed to seek her out this was not always possible. Eliza herself noticed little of this. When she left the breakfast-room she went immediately to Sophia's chamber where she proceeded to sit, sometimes with the maid, sometimes alone, watching intently every fluctuation in the girl's condition. By evening she was concerned. Sophia, although indeed aching and feverish, had remained lucid most of the day, but as the light began to fail she became hot and dry, tossing restlessly beneath the covers. Eliza, who had thought the girl asleep, was startled when she cried out loudly for her father and alarmed when her soothing words produced a wild look of non-recognition in the girl's cornflower eyes.

'Papa!' Sophia cried again, sobbing dryly in her throat. 'Why will you not let him come? I know he loves me!'

'Of course, darling,' Eliza murmured, bathing the hot brow with a little vinegar. 'I'm sure he will not be long.'

The reassurance seemed to calm her a little and she lay back upon the pillows with closed eyes, but when Eliza moved towards the door she started up again, her cheeks flaming and eyes hollow, to cry out pitifully: 'Lizzy? Don't go!'

'I'm not going, dearest,' Eliza assured her, returning at once and surreptitiously pulling the bell.

Sophia lay down again but continued to watch Eliza as though she thought she might disappear. Eliza's summons produced a maid within a minute or two and under Sophia's watchful gaze Eliza quietly told the girl to send for the doctor. When she turned back to the bed Sophia's head had fallen to one side and she seemed amazingly to have dropped into an uneasy doze.

For the next half hour Eliza's eyes did not leave the girl's face. Sophia did not wake again but continued to toss restlessly, murmuring

149

unintelligibly from time to time. When a gentle tap came on the door Eliza started but Sophia did not react, so she crept quietly across thick carpet and opened it gently.

It was Mr Foxcroft. So surprised was she that her jaw dropped slightly and she did not resist when he took her arm and drew her into the corridor. She noticed then that Mrs Foxcroft's maid was at his side and was in fact entering the room at that very moment. She made a protest but it was ineffectual; she found herself drawn away down the passage.

'Dr Glover is out at a delivery,' he told her soberly. 'He'll be here as soon as he can, I'm sure. In the meantime, Miss Woodeforde, have you eaten today?'

'Eaten? I don't know, but sir, I cannot leave her! She is not herself.'

Mr Foxcroft stopped and stared down at her, his dark eyes momentarily unfathomable. 'There is some danger?'

'I know not indeed!' She stared anxiously up at him and said with forced calmness: 'She talks wildly and does not always know me.'

For a moment the gentleman did not answer. Finally, and not looking at her, he said briskly: 'There is nothing you can do. Millie is quite capable. You are exhausted, Miss Woodeforde, and I insist on your having something to eat. I know where Dr Glover is and shall ride for him.'

'You?' Eliza's tone clearly showed her

disbelief.

'Yes.' He smiled ruefully. 'My presence might serve to convince him of the urgency of the matter.'

She eyed him dubiously and said: 'I believe it is raining!'

'If it is I am sure you will consider it suitable penance for my sins.'

Eliza was forced to smile but said: 'If you may only bring him back, Mr Foxcroft—!'

He met her eyes gravely for a moment and then said briskly: 'My mother dines at seven, Miss Woodeforde. She would appreciate it greatly if you joined her.' And then he was gone. Perplexed, Eliza stared after his rapidly retreating back, at a loss to define the oddness of his humour.

But when he returned, rather more than two hours later and soaked to his skin, he had brought the doctor and earned her gratitude. As long as the doctor was with his patient she barely gave him a thought, but when she saw how very wet he had become and how his coat dripped water as he stood outside the sick-room her conscience was stirred and she flushed slightly as she said: 'Sir, had you not better change? You may be healthy, to be sure, but nothing is more foolhardy than standing about in wet clothes!'

A smile momentarily lit his eyes and he bowed. 'Very well, ma'am, no doubt you are correct!' And he left her again, before she had time to express the gratitude she truly felt.

After that she did not see him for two days. Sophia, while not in any immediate danger, continued to alarm her nurses, and Eliza, although reluctant at first, was grateful after a sleepless night to accept the help of Mary in the sick-room. A few moments had served to convince her of the girl's capability and, while she did not care to be absent more than a few hours, it enabled her to snatch some much needed rest on the truckle-bed set up in the dressing-room. As she ate all her meals upstairs, she knew very little of what went on around her; for although Jemima Stanley appeared occasionally, to regale her with tales of Carleton's distraction and Mr Foxcroft's exasperation, she was able to pay very little attention and was merely relieved that Mrs Foxcroft's kindness and understanding meant she did not have to be present at all times.

Snatching a turn about the shrubbery late one afternoon she had come upon Mr Foxcroft by accident, although he seemed to have been looking for her. This impression was strengthened when he turned and walked at her side; but he seemed, strangely for him, to be at a loss for words, Although she sensed him to be thinking deeply, they proceeded for several minutes in complete silence before he turned to her and asked whether she thought there was any real danger still to be apprehended.

She looked at him in surprise. 'Surely, Mr Foxcroft, you must know as well as I how things stand? Does not Dr Glover give you a regular report?'

'He does of course, but it occurs to me that you, being so familiar with her, might be able to give a more accurate impression.'

'Perhaps; I know not.' She hesitated a moment and then said: 'I am sure, sir, if you wished, you might visit her occasionally.'

He glanced down at her briefly and answered shortly: 'No, I do not think so, Miss Woodeforde.'

'Afraid of infection, sir? There is little danger of that, I am told.'

He was frowning now and she knew he could not have missed the scorn in her tone and while she remembered her gratitude of two days ago she could not be sorry.

'I wish I knew, ma'am, what I had done to give you such a poor opinion of me.'

She was startled. Mr Foxcroft had stopped suddenly and turned to face her, a strangeness of expression in his eyes that made her almost fear him. 'I?' she answered weakly.

'Yes, indeed! Since our first meeting you have been determined to despise me, determined at all costs to prevent my marriage to Miss Crawley! Tell me, Miss Woodeforde, what is it that puts you so above me and my family that you wish for nought to do with us, that the merest suggestion of an alliance is poison?'

Eliza stood very still. He had gone very white, she noticed curiously, and the blackness of his hair and brows stood out harshly against his skin. He was speaking again, but she barely heard him. It was sufficient to know that it was simply more of the same. For as long as he berated her she remained silent, but when finally, exhausted of words, he stopped, she drew breath deeply and said in a voice that trembled slightly: 'How strange it is to hear you talk so! I declare I could almost laugh!' She did so, but it was a feeble attempt. 'You ask me why I despise you, sir, then I shall tell you. I did not need to know you to be aware of your reputation. Have I not a right to be concerned for Miss Crawley's happiness? Have you not possessed a string of mistresses, Mr Foxcroft, even setting them up in some style in fashionable London mansions? How was I to be content with such an alliance for the friend I value most? Why should I stand idly by while her father and you conspire to condemn her to a life of misery? For such it would be, Mr Foxcroft! You might intend to mend your ways, I know not, but good intentions never endure, and certainly, I am sure, not yours!'

His lip curled. 'I did not know, Miss Woodeforde, when I spoke of your dislike, how intense that was. I suppose I must thank you for so enlightening me. I own, I had thought, over the past few days, that you had come to dislike me less, even to care about me a little, but I see now that I was mistaken.'

Her brain whirled unpleasantly, but Eliza forced a laugh. 'In the past few days, Mr Foxcroft, your character has been more revealed to me than ever before!' She drew breath in an attempt to still the uncomfortable pounding in her chest and plunged on: 'You speak to me of my superiority, but what of yours, Mr Foxcroft? Can you tell me why your family are at such pains to disrupt your engagement, even going to the extreme of inviting that unfortunate fellow to make calf's eyes at her? Can you deny that, between you, you have done enough to send Miss Crawley even to the brink of death?'

She barely knew what she was saying. Hunger and anxiety made her giddy; she swayed a little and for a moment thought she would faint. Mr Foxcroft's figure faded briefly and she had an impression of his starting towards her. Then her vision cleared and she steadied herself.

Mr Foxcroft's expression had been one of alarm and he had sense enough to realize that she knew not what she was saying. When he saw she was recovered, however, he assumed an expression of mild amusement and Eliza, who had thought to goad him, felt strangely let down when he simply turned on his heel and left her.

CHAPTER EIGHT

Sophia was now on the mend. Her fever reached its zenith and abated, leaving her weakened and restless, desiring one moment to leave her bed and the next to return to it. Of Mr Foxcroft Eliza had no sight and was glad until she discovered he had left Ingham. This knowledge caused her some dismay and, combined with her growing restlessness at her position, served to make her heartily depressed. Among her companions at Ingham there was no one with whom she could converse, for business had taken Miss Stanley from them also. Since she had little inclination for the conversation of either Lady Ludlow or her mother she was glad to escape into the grounds, leaving Sophia to the companionship and care of Mary and the doting adoration of Mr Davenham. The propriety of this was doubtful, she had to admit, but her feelings on the matter of Sophia's marriage were so confused she desired nothing less than to be subjected to the girl's languishing complaints. Mary too had proved herself a far more appropriate companion than she, and nothing, Eliza judged, would serve better to bring her charge about than the flattering attentions of a personable, if indeed bird-witted, young gentleman. That Sophia should ever encourage him never entered her head. Eliza saw him as a good-natured, moon-struck halfling about whom no one could have a serious thought. If Sophia, when they met, proved listless and non-communicative, preferring, it seemed, the conversation and companionship of her contemporaries, Eliza could not complain. The girl had been too long from young people and the listlessness, well, it was doubtless caused by the lingering discomforts of her recent malady.

Consequently Eliza took herself frequently to the stables, wearing a shabby, well-darned riding-dress she took care no one but the groom should see, and amused herself by riding into the estate on one of the well-tempered mares it pleased Mr Foxcroft to keep, presumably for ladies of a somewhat different order from her.

The two matrons of Ingham, however, were regarding the progress of Carleton's infatuation with a far less disinterested eye. Mrs Foxcroft's early disapproval of her daughter's tactics had suffered a sharp change when she realized the hopelessness of such a match and while she was careful that no part in it should fall to herself she nevertheless took a grim satisfaction from observing the look of slavish adoration on Carleton's Grecian features and the delicate flush that rose to Sophia's otherwise pallid complexion whenever he entered the room.

All this Mary observed in increasing alarm and indignation. While never for a moment doubting her cousin's integrity, or indeed Sophia's faith to Mr Foxcroft, she yet found herself incensed and consequently sought out her mother at the earliest opportunity.

'Carleton making a cake of himself?' repeated the dowager, not raising her head from her writing-desk. 'Of course I have seen it! When did he not, pray, over some foolish scheme or other? I'm sure it is no more than we should expect from a son of Celia Calderbeck. A niminy-piminy creature she always was, even in her youth, and age has given her no more sense than a sparrow!'

'But, Mama, do you not think it inappropriate for Carleton to be displaying himself so? Miss Crawley is, after all, promised to my uncle!'

Lady Ludlow eyed her daughter with impatience. 'I had not forgot, my love, I assure you! And I would have thought you possessed more sense than to stand in your cousin's way as you are perpetually doing. That governess-creature has more the idea, I can assure you! What a feather in her cap it would be to see her beloved pupil the future Lady Ludlow of Mandrath! Though I must admit,' she added, frowning heavily, 'that it seems most unfair that such a perfect widgeon should succeed me! I'm sure she is worse even than that creature who calls herself Lady Ludlow now!'

Mary scowled in a manner that would certainly have drawn her mother's reproof had she seen it. 'Mama, I do not think you hear yourself. Why do you wish to serve my uncle such a back-handed turn?'

Lady Ludlow sanded the sheet and laughed shallowly. 'Back-handed? Mary, my dear child, I am taking care of his interests, you may be assured! How long, do you suppose, could such a marriage last? Within a month Julius would be back to his old ways and you may take it from me, child, that they were nothing to be proud of and nothing to subject a poor, innocent child like Miss Crawley to.'

'His mistresses, you mean, and the gambling?'

'Mary!' Lady Ludlow rolled her eyes heavenwards. 'I know not where you had such notions! And if you scowl like that you will be a wrinkled prune before you are twenty and then what shall I do to turn you off?'

But Mary's frown did not lift. She sat down upon the edge of the bed and contemplated her mother gravely. 'Mama, has it not occurred to you that Uncle Julius might love Miss Crawley?'

Her laugh genuine, Lady Ludlow eyed her daughter with incredulity writ large across her broad, powdered face. 'Lord, child, where had you such a notion? You must stop reading penny novelettes if this is all you learn. Besides, if he dotes so greatly upon her why did he never once visit her when she was ill? And why, may I ask, has he fled to London as soon as all danger is passed?'

To this Mary had no answer. Feeling strangely battered and depressed she excused herself her mother's presence and went to find a more tolerant ear for her opinions. But Miss Woodeforde, worn out by the exigencies of a day's ride, had retired early to her bed, so Mary's confidences were obliged to await another day for their hearing.

On the following morning, however, Lady Ludlow took affairs more firmly into her own hands. By the greasing of several palms she discovered that Sophia had declined Eliza's cordial invitation to take a gentle ride about the grounds and when she had seen the pestilential Miss Woodeforde ride from the precincts of the house she set about putting her plan into action. She had already suggested to her mother that Mary might benefit from a little conversation with her revered grandmama and now contrived to get the girl summoned to the old woman's bed-chamber in a manner rather too peremptory to be refused. Having bribed Carleton's valet to rouse him two hours earlier than usual, she took herself to her own apartments and consequently was well out of the way when Carleton made his yawning entry to the breakfast-room.

The sight of Miss Crawley toying with her

bread and butter quite drove from his head the indignation he had felt on discovering the mysterious aberration of his valet. With an access of good-humour he resolved to forgive the fellow and seated himself with a smile of utter happiness upon the smoothness of his perfect features.

'I say!' he exclaimed, carving himself a large wedge of under-cooked beef. 'This is above all things great!'

Sophia, confused at finding herself alone with a gentleman, bent her head over her plate and agreed that it was.

'Do you know,' continued Carleton, not noticing her embarrassment, 'I had almost resolved to dispense with my valet? Quite true! Though where I should have found anyone to match him the Lord knows, for he has a way with a boot I've yet to see equalled.' He thought for a moment and then said: 'No, that ain't true, for Jameson, Mr Foxcroft's man, gets a depth to his shine that Collins can't!' He extended his leg as he spoke and examined the gloss on his hessians with a frowning eye and then, seemingly aware of Miss Crawley's bewildered expression, grinned suddenly and added: 'Breakfast! Woke me two hours early, you see. I had thought to let him go, but now—!'

Comprehending, Sophia smiled shyly and lowered her eyes once more to her plate.

For some minutes they continued in silence.

161

It was borne upon Carleton now that never since their first meeting in the shrubbery had he found himself quite alone with the young lady of his dreams, a realization which robbed him of all powers of conversation. Finally, when Sophia had finished and rose from the table, he jumped up himself, ignoring the chair that crashed over, and presented himself in her path.

'Mr Davenham!' Sophia exclaimed, her colour fading rapidly. 'Whatever is the matter?'

Carleton shook his head dumbly and ran his fingers through his hair, thus destroying the work of half an hour.

'Mr Davenham, if you have nothing to say please let me pass!'

'Miss Crawley, I must speak with you!' Carleton managed at last, though his voice was so husky it was a wonder she understood him.

'Talk to me?' Sophia repeated faintly, swaying slightly and clutching desperately at a chair-back. 'What about?'

Carleton swallowed. 'Mr Foxcroft,' he uttered, his voice a high, unmanly squeak.

'Oh.' Sophia swayed again and Carleton, recovering his wits in time to steady her, solicitously dragged out a chair and seated her in it. 'Please, Mr Davenham, do not!'

'Do not? Miss Crawley, you do not understand!'

'Oh, I do, I do! It is you who do not

162

understand! It is all quite, quite hopeless!' Carleton did not know the novel from which this affecting line was taken, but when Sophia dropped her head into her hands and began to sob something stirred in his memory and he pulled out his own, exquisite silk handkerchief. Righting his maltreated chair, he sat down and, tapping Sophia on the arm, dumbly held out the square of cream-coloured silk.

The offer brought on a fresh bout of weeping, but she took the kerchief gratefully and defiantly blew her nose. 'Forgive me, Mr Davenham, it is so stupid of me!'

'No, no!' Carleton assured her, sensing the inadequacy of his words. He watched her for a moment longer and then said: 'Is it Uncle Julius?'

Sophia did not answer at once. When she did it was to repeat her earlier statement: 'So stupid of me!'

Carleton pondered. There was more to this, he felt, than met the eye. 'Do you not wish to marry him, then?' he asked finally.

Sophia shook her head. 'We do not suit!'

'Oh.' Carleton nodded wisely. 'Then do not marry him, Miss Crawley, if you do not suit.'

'But I *have* to!' Sophia cried, smothering her face once more with the fine silk. 'He has made such . . . promises, that Papa will not countenance my refusal. It would break his heart!'

'*His* heart!' Carleton ejaculated, roused at

163

last to volubility. 'I tell you, Miss Crawley, if you marry my uncle it will break mine!'

Sophia stopped crying for a moment to whisper: 'Truly?'

'Most certainly,' he assured her, though his colour rushed up alarmingly upon the words.

'Oh!' Sophia breathed, her face wreathed suddenly in smiles. 'I so hoped it would be so!'

'Well, it is,' Carleton responded, scowling heavily at the floor. 'Since that first moment you seemed like . . . an angel!'

'Oh, so did you!' Miss Crawley exclaimed rapturously, the situation reminding her forcibly of just such an affecting scene in *Angelina's Promise*.

Carleton, finding nothing amiss with this equation, was moved to look at her. 'I did? I say!'

He tried to take her hands at this point but Sophia resisted saying huskily: 'Carleton, we must not!'

'Must not?' he exclaimed, rather loudly. 'Gammon!'

He made to take her hands again but she pulled them away and finally was obliged to sit on them to prevent him. 'No, no, Carleton, you forget!' She raised anguished eyes to his face and whispered, as had Angelina before her: 'I am promised!'

Carleton frowned fearfully. 'I shall not permit it,' he announced finally.

'Oh, but there is nothing you can do!'

Sophia told him, pathetically sniffing. 'My father is so determined I shall marry Julius that I cannot disobey him!'

'Cannot?'

She stared into his eyes. 'Would you disobey your father?'

His scowl deepening, Carleton thought of his lordship, the scornful way he greeted his son's fanciful whims and the peremptory manner in which he dismissed them. 'I suppose I would not,' he admitted, the scowl giving way to an expression of deep gloom. 'Whatever shall we do?'

'I shall marry Mr Foxcroft and you, in a little while, will marry some heiress, I dare say, and forget about me.'

'Never!' declared Carleton, revolted. 'If I cannot marry you I shall never marry!'

'Won't you? Will you not be very lonely?'

'I dare say, but I shall have my dogs.'

Sophia nodded and they sat on together, each brooding on a future of misery.

'We shall see each other sometimes, though,' Carleton pronounced at last.

'Yes, but never alone.'

'Never?'

Sophia shook her head. 'It would be far too dangerous! Only think how *angry* everyone would be if they had the smallest notion of how we felt!'

'Lord, yes!' exclaimed Carleton, much struck. 'I dare say they would send me away to some dashed god-forsaken place.'

Sophia nodded. 'Almost certainly, I believe. Why, Eliza's father was sent to India just for falling in love.'

'Really?' Carleton exclaimed, appalled.

'Oh yes! Eliza said he loved a beautiful young woman who was unfortunately betrothed to his elder brother. She is Lady Carlow now.'

'But sent to India?' Carleton repeated, horrified.

'Oh yes! And he caught some terrible disease and died, *years* later! It must have been *awful!*'

'Awful!' Carleton agreed thoughtfully. 'Do you know, I cannot believe India would suit me at all.'

'No! And if you died I should kill myself too! So you see, no one must ever know!'

'No!' He pondered the fate of the unknown Clarence Woodeforde a moment longer and then said: 'We must not see each other alone again.'

'No,' Sophia agreed and the thought prompted her to catch up Carleton's handkerchief. After a few seconds she calmed herself with an effort and held out to Carleton the sodden, crumpled silk.

'No!' exclaimed Carleton, his expression worthy of Sir Lancelot. 'You must keep it.'

'Oh!' The tears began again, but Sophia continued to stare mistily at her love. 'I shall treasure it always!'

Carleton smiled bravely. 'Whenever I see it I shall know you have not forgotten me,' he told her solemnly.

'Yes!' Sophia breathed, tucking the scrap of material reverentially into her reticule. Resolutely she stood up and held out her hand. 'Goodbye, Mr Davenham,' she said. Carleton rose too. For a moment he stared at her from his superior height and then, with an access of gallantry, took her hand and kissed it. In a moment he had turned on his heel and, with his head erect and eye quite dry, left the room. A Galahad would have been proud of him.

* * *

It was not often that a hostess had been able to accuse Julius Foxcroft of insulting behaviour. To be sure, he could deliver the most damning set-down one had heard if he so chose and many a young buck had retired in disorder on demanding the name of his latest style in neckcloth arrangement. But an insult such as the cut direct to one of the patronesses of Almack's, or a departure from an engagement barely ten minutes after he had arrived, was something he had never committed, or at least never until that fateful night in February 1814. The ball had been an important affair. To be sure, Mr Foxcroft had arrived in London too late to answer the invitation that stood with the others on the mantleshelf, too late in fact to do more than disregard the fatigues of travel and exchange top-boots and breeches for the splendours of evening-dress. He had not even intended going out, for indeed his journeying to London at all had been the action of a desperate man, one anxious to escape a situation that had threatened to send him to bedlam. But on his arrival in Berkeley Square something had happened. He had remembered the engagement in time and, knowing Lady Coldmain would certainly forgive his recent silence if he graced her ball with his presence, he had sallied forth, looking upon the evening's entertainment rather as a drowning man sees the outstretched hand before him. And yet within ten minutes he had departed from Lady Coldmain's glittering ballroom, ignoring the smiles and bows of the Princess Esterhazy, wife of the Austrian Ambassador, and Almack's most formidable patroness. Grasping hat and cane, he had virtually fled from the house, leaving his hostess speechless and the whole company within a very few minutes to buzz with speculation. As to what had caused this departure from the norm no one seemed to know. One moment the gentleman had been dancing, and with the young lady who promised to be the prize of the season, seventeen, beautiful and the heiress to a fortune. He had not quite left her standing in the centre of the floor, which would have been unforgivable, but he had escorted the child to her mama in the middle of a quadrille and with barely a word had left the room. The heiress had suffered a fit of hysterics, while her mama declared that that 'insufferable man' had ruined her whole season. Lady Coldmain and the Princess Esterhazy had merely exchanged glances, but the future looked black indeed for Mr Foxcroft should he ever try to set foot in Almack's again.

Fortunately he seemed quite unaware of the terrible fate that awaited him. Summoning a hackney, he had returned at once to Berkeley Square and it was only his recollection of the lateness of the hour that had prevented his setting out for Berkshire at once. He issued some very terse instructions to the skeleton staff in attendance, leaving them to set in motion preparations for the imminent arrival of a new mistress.

CHAPTER NINE

Mr Foxcroft's sudden and unexpected return to Ingham barely four days after he had left could not be said to have caused delight. His carriage, rolling somewhat faster than was safe up the finely gravelled drive, was first observed

169

by Mary and her exclamation ' 'Tis my uncle!' served very well to jerk Miss Crawley from her reverie. She sprang to her feet, her eyes wild, and cried hysterically: 'I cannot!' With that she turned in some haste, tripped over her trailing shawl, caught it up and hurried from the room. She encountered in the hall a grim-faced Carleton dressed for riding in top-boots. His expression had lifted slightly at the sight of her, but dropped ludicrously when she gasped out her appalling information.

'I shall tell him all!' he announced, struggling to inject some firmness into his voice.

'Oh no! Carleton, *pray* do not! *Promise* me!'

'Very well,' he agreed, not a little relieved to be deprived of this unpleasant office. 'But should he trouble you—'

'Oh yes, yes, but I must hurry! Only listen, there is his carriage!'

To be sure the crunch of wheels could indeed be heard, and in a moment too Sterne appeared, straightening his cravat prior to greeting his master. Sophia had already fled upstairs but Carleton hesitated a moment before turning and striding purposefully in the direction of the stables. In spite of the promise he had given, he could not but feel himself to be ignobly weak. A confrontation, he suspected, would be far from pleasant and yet—Mentally he shook himself. How many times had he considered just such a

170

conversation? Already he could see the derision in the dark eyes and feel the merciless lash of his tongue. Foxcroft, he was convinced, would then tell it all to his father, who would almost certainly dispatch him to India upon the next packet. He would have to shoot himself and what possible good could he do for Miss Crawley if he were dead? It was, as he had already told himself a thousand times, all too hopeless to be considered. He had reached the cobbled stable-yard by this time but barely sensed it, jumping when the groom's boy touched his forelock and addressed him. He recovered himself, however, and requested his mount and in a minute or two had ridden from the yard.

Mr Foxcroft's countenance as he handed his hat and gloves to his butler gave little indication of the exigencies of his journey. Indeed there was a decidedly wicked gleam in his eye as he demanded to know where the devil everybody was hiding. Upon the intelligence that Mr Davenham had but a moment earlier departed for a ride and that Miss Crawley had retreated to her chamber he gave a satisfied grunt and announced that he would have a glass of madeira sent to his library. Here, still in his travel-stained breeches of the palest biscuit, he ensconced himself for the next two hours, to emerge apparently considerably refreshed and resolved. Since it was by now very nearly dinner-time haste was required and he mounted the stairs two at a time to reach his chamber. His valet, who had been observing the lateness of the hour for some little time, was fully prepared, dragging off his master's boots and relieving him of his coat with a speed many would envy. But Mr Foxcroft himself was no dawdler. Not for him the hours spent on the tying of a cravat. Indeed the fashionable world would have been considerably surprised to learn that rarely more than two attempts were ever made on the complicated arrangements of his neckcloth and that the small selection of fobs and seals on his waistband was made more by chance than careful consideration. Even so he was the last to descend to the drawing-room. The company, having been apprised of his presence, had awaited his arrival, but it could not be said that his final appearance was greeted with any marked degree of enthusiasm. It was plain that Mrs Foxcroft felt herself somewhat put out at being obliged to wait and her daughter, ever of uncertain temper, merely regarded the event as a further instance of her younger brother's mammoth inconsideration. If Mr Foxcroft's glance travelled to Miss Woodeforde or Miss Crawley neither knew of it, for both had seen fit to engage in a fervent conversation about the merits of muslins. Mr Davenham uttered not a word, his usually vacuous countenance

172

distorted by a huge and seemingly fearful frown. Only Mary greeted her uncle with unaffected pleasure and some relief. Undaunted by the chilliness of his reception Mr Foxcroft's good humour was such that Carleton, unfortunately catching the gentleman's eye during the meal, was cast into a fit of terror by the sparkle therein. Being inclined to think his uncle some kind of demigod whose powers were unimaginable, terrible and inevitable, he saw at once that his dreadful secret had been discovered and that a horrible revenge was even now being planned. He risked a glance across the table at Miss Crawley and saw, with ready sympathy, a similar fear in her large eyes. Mr Foxcroft had inquired very kindly after her health, informing her that she appeared in fine bloom, words that drove the last vestige of colour from her cheeks. She looked anything but blooming, Carleton thought compassionately and considered that it only went to show how amazingly callous and unfeeling Mr Foxcroft could be. And it seemed too, to Carleton's labouring intelligence, that other members of the party were not wholly delighted by Mr Foxcroft's presence. Even Carleton was not blind to the looks of scarcely veiled hatred cast at her brother by Lady Ludlow; while Miss Woodeforde, whose spirit he had come to respect, seemed as cowed almost as Sophia and he. Only Mary appeared cheerful,

Carleton thought dismally. Indeed her efforts at conversation simply had to be admired, hampered as they were by the apparent inability of anyone else to utter a civil sentence.

When the meal finally dragged itself to an end Mr Davenham felt an unutterable relief. The ladies were rising to leave the chamber and he would have followed, had not Mr Foxcroft, by a muttered word to his butler, indicated that he wished to break a bottle of port. With a depression of spirit Mr Davenham sank back into his seat. As a rule Mr Foxcroft did not delay long after the ladies, perhaps because he found the young man's conversation desultory, but today, Carleton predicted gloomily, he would probably last the rest of the evening. And so indeed it seemed. Mr Foxcroft had pushed back his chair and stretched his long legs before him and Carleton's tentative suggestion that the ladies might expect them fell on stony ground.

'Come now, my good fellow,' Mr Foxcroft exclaimed, his tone gently mocking, 'surely you will not fail me? I had thought you enjoyed a glass of port and this, as you must know, is quite excellent!'

So Carleton, his misery writ large, obliged his host, his unfortunate brain already wondering which death would be most painless. After a while, however, he began to think his fears had been groundless. Surely the gentleman was being far too kind to him. Of course the mocking gleam had not quite vanished from those dark eyes, but Carleton did begin to wonder whether he had not perhaps over-dramatised the situation.

This was an impression Mr Foxcroft had been at some pains to give. Since encountering the young man that evening the light in which he was regarded had seemed plain. Carleton considered him little less than an ogre and was terrified. While this necessarily amused the hard-hearted Mr Foxcroft, he had to admit it was prejudicial to his cause and consequently he had been at some pains to set his guest at ease. When Carleton seemed finally to relax Mr Foxcroft did not feel he could take a great deal of credit, since he had seen to it that Carleton's glass was never less than half-full. Now, however, he dismissed the hovering servant and caught up the decanter himself. Carleton drunk would be no use to him at all, but what he had seen of the young man led him to believe he possessed an unexpectedly steady head. He refilled his glass therefore and said: 'Tell me, my dear fellow, do you think my future bride has quite recovered from her malady?'

Carleton choked upon his port. Mr Foxcroft, patient while the coughs subsided, could not congratulate himself on his subtlety, but pressed on nevertheless.

'I own, I thought her a trifle pale tonight,

did not you? I hope there is no real cause for concern.'

He bent his head over his snuff-box as he spoke lest Carleton should think his question too pointed. And now the young man was emboldened to answer. 'I thought her pale, yes.'

'But a cause for concern?' Mr Foxcroft raised his head and contemplated him gravely. 'You have been much in her company, I believe. Pray tell me what you think.'

'I think . . . she has not completely recovered, sir.'

Mr Foxcroft nodded slowly. 'Perhaps Ingham does not agree with her,' he suggested. 'I truly hope it is not so, for I had intended that we should spend much of our time here.' He sighed and leant back in his chair with his hands behind his head. 'Tell me, Carleton, do you not think her a divine creature? I was fortunate, was I not, to trap her like that?' He glanced covertly at Carleton and saw him arrested. 'Of course, I could have done nothing without the father. If you ever have an eye to a wench, my boy, that's the only way to do it. Turn her father up sweet, promise him a handsome settlement and the thing's done.' He glanced at Carleton again and then shut his eyes. 'Of course in my case the matter was easy. You'd never dream it, I know, Sophy being such an angel, but her father rides devilish rusty! The most purse-pinching, knaggy old gagger it was ever my misfortune to come across. Or fortune, perhaps, for there's no knowing whether he'd have taken me otherwise! Do you know, Davenham,' here he sat up and eyed the young man frankly, 'I truly think he'd have wed the girl to some thatch-gallows if he only had funds enough.' He contemplated Carleton a moment longer and then caught up his snuff-box again. 'Of course I shall do the right thing by his daughter, such a pretty widgeon that she is! And, between you and me, dear fellow,' here he delivered himself of an outrageous wink, 'she'll not be forever nabbing the rust at any gentleman's pastime I might indulge in.' With an air of slight drunkenness he succeeded in opening the tiny snuff-box, but when he lurched across the table towards the young man Carleton stood up abruptly. Mr Foxcroft eyed him in apparent amazement as he straightened his cravat, seemingly wrestling for command of himself. Finally, with an expression of scorn upon his face, he managed to say: 'I believe I shall join the ladies after all.'

Mr Foxcroft, supporting his chin upon his hands, watched bemusedly as the young man left the room. Then, as the door clicked shut, he sat up and fingered the little snuff-box thoughtfully. 'I wonder,' he murmured softly, 'did I overplay my hand?' He gave the matter a moment's consideration and then, with a sober steadiness, refilled his glass from the decanter.

177

Mr Davenham, bursting into the blue drawing-room, was obliged to curb the urgency and impatience that had driven him. For indeed all five ladies present had raised amazed eyes to his face, causing him to grin somewhat sheepishly and flush.

'For heaven's sake, Carleton, do sit down!' exclaimed Lady Ludlow exasperatedly. 'And where is Julius, might I ask?'

Carleton sat down and then stood up again to release the tails of his coat. 'Mr Foxcroft is in the dining-room.'

Lady Ludlow eyed her nephew severely. 'And why, pray, has he elected not to join us?'

Carleton's flush deepened. Glancing desperately at his cousin Mary he seemed for some reason tongue-tied and was consequently greatly relieved when Mrs Foxcroft, from the depths of her chair, stated: 'If Julius chooses not to join us I do not believe the matter needs discussing. In any event I am tired. Mary, my dear, would you ring for Millie?'

Miserably Carleton realised he was going to have to wait before making his urgent communications. To be sure, Sophia had looked considerably startled when he had burst upon them, but she was now conversing with Miss Woodeforde prior, it seemed, to retiring for the night. He tried vainly to catch her eye for some minutes until it became plain that his actions had been observed by everyone except the lady in question. There seemed to be nothing for it but to retire, which he did, with as much grace as he could muster.

The following morning, however, Fate seemed to smile upon him. Recalling an earlier occasion, he ignored all the dictates of his body and brain to rise at ten o'clock; hoping, as once before, to find Miss Crawley in the breakfast-room. He did not, for it was deserted, but, recalling that he had no longer anything to lose, he boldly inquired of the servant whether he had seen Miss Crawley that morning. The fellow had, it seemed, for she was walking outside the window. With scarcely a second glance at the fine rib of beef that lay untouched upon the table Carleton rose and threw open the breakfast-room window. It was an easy task to step over the low sill and the sinking of his highly polished hessians into the soft earth outside was but a small price to pay for the vista he received. Miss Crawley was barely three yards away, walking in a listless fashion, her shawl trailing unheeded on the gravel of the path. As he stepped out of the flower-bed she turned her head, blushing becomingly at the sight of his ardent features.

'Oh Carleton! I so hoped I would see you today!' Two steps brought him to her side and he clasped her hands in a lover-like manner that brought a sparkle to her blue eyes. 'I have been so worried for you! Mr Foxcroft—he seemed so strange last night, I was quite frightened!'

179

'So was I!' Carleton responded with some feeling. He recollected their position, however, and turned her back along the path. 'It was monstrous strange, I can assure you. Do you know, Julius was quite in his cups? I declare I've never seen him in such a case before!'

'You mean—inebriated?' Sophia was clearly revolted.

'Undoubtedly, but do you know, it was a vastly good thing? He said such things to me, Sophy! And I have decided!'

Sophia's eyes grew large. 'What?' she whispered.

'You are going to marry me,' he told her firmly.

'Marry? Oh, but I can't!' She had paled as she spoke and now stood trembling beside him, tears starting in her eyes.

'Yes, you can, for he showed me the way. We're going to run away.'

'*Run away?*' Sophia echoed, horrified. 'You mean *elope*? Carleton, I should die for shame!'

'No, of course not! I could no more do so myself! No, I have it all decided. We shall go to your father.'

Sophia's eyes grew large. 'My *father*? But that is impossible! He would beat me and lock me up and send me back to Mr Foxcroft, sure as anything!'

But Carleton shook his head firmly. 'No, he won't, Sophy. And do you know why? I'll tell you. Actually it was Mr Foxcroft himself showed me the way!'

'How? I don't understand!'

'Sophy, what is it your father liked best about your marrying Mr Foxcroft?'

She shook her head bewilderedly.

'The settlements! Did he not promise your father something handsome for you?'

'I think so, but—'

'Don't you see? When I inherit I shall have far more money than Foxcroft, and Mandrath too! And what's more,' he added, smiling sheepishly, 'I shall be My Lord!'

Sophia was staring at her handsome swain with a curious expression in her wonderful eyes. 'You truly think—oh, if only it might be true!'

'Of course it is!' he assured her with some conviction. 'I am certain of it.'

'But Carleton, then we can be together!' She held out her hands to him again and he clasped them firmly, but of a sudden her ecstatic expression faded and she said hollowly: 'But, Carleton, how can we escape? Mr Foxcroft will never let me go!'

Mr Davenham's face fell ludicrously. 'No, by God, he won't! And Miss Woodeforde would not help us either. She probably thinks me some sort of sapskull, not good enough for you.'

While Sophia hotly denied this she could not but agree that Eliza would probably oppose their flight.

'And so would my cousin,' Carleton continued gloomily. 'She is forever trying to keep you from me!'

'I know!' Sophia concurred with some feeling. 'In fact,' she added, with a furtive glance over her shoulder, 'I almost expect her to come upon us at any moment!'

Carleton frowned heavily. 'Well,' he said, trying to inject some firmness into his voice, 'we must just run away. Under cover of dark,' he added obscurely.

'In the dark?' Sophia looked anxiously into her lover's frowning countenance. 'Carleton, I don't think that such a good idea! If we were caught, only think how very—Bad it would look!'

'Yes, you're right. And, while there would of course be nothing Improper, I should not care to have anyone ever think it.'

'No, indeed,' agreed Sophia, blushing to the roots of her hair.

Carleton cleared his throat and, his face only slightly reddened, continued: 'I see what we must do. I shall—somehow—possess myself of a carriage. You must just go for a walk, only I do think you ought not to carry too big a valise, in case anyone should see you.'

'A v . . . valise?' Sophia's face fell. 'Carleton, I do not think I can take a valise at all! Will it matter very much?'

'Of course not!' exclaimed Carleton. 'To be

sure, it would look a trifle odd, would it not?' He frowned heavily. 'And now I come to think of it I had better leave everything also or we should be in the suds!' He stared warmly down at his love. 'How fortunate you are so much more up to snuff than I am! I'm sure without you I should be quite at point-non-plus!'

'Oh no!' Sophia disclaimed hurriedly. 'You are *far* cleverer than I am! Only think! But for you we should never see each other again!'

'No!' agreed Carleton, much struck by this evidence of his own brilliance. 'So this is what you must do. Tomorrow morning go for a walk.' He glanced at the flimsy shawl she trailed behind her. 'Only, do you think you might wear a warmer wrap? The drive, you know—'

'Oh, yes! But, Carleton, how will you get us a carriage?'

'Don't worry about that,' Carleton responded, scowling fiercely. 'Just be at the lodge-gates by . . .' he thought rapidly, 'ten o'clock.'

Sophia nodded, more than content with this arrangement of affairs. 'I only wish I did not have to deceive them all so!'

'Yes!' Mr Davenham agreed with some feeling.

'Especially Eliza! She will be so hurt!'

Carleton patted her hand comfortingly. 'She'll understand when you can explain it to her.'

'Do you think so?' Sophia asked wretchedly. 'It seems so deceitful!'

Mr Davenham frowned heavily, his Apollonian features painfully corrugated. 'It is difficult, but—' His brow cleared as by magic. 'You must write her a letter!'

'A letter?'

'Yes,' he said, nodding decisively. 'Then you may explain and perhaps she will not be so hurt.'

'Yes,' Sophia said slowly, 'only she must not find it too soon!'

'No. Perhaps if you put it in a drawer,' Carleton suggested, somewhat vaguely.

'Perhaps. Well,' Sophia said brightly, 'I shall find a way.' She glanced fearfully back down the path and said: 'But I think we should part now, don't you? Only think how dreadful it would be for someone to see us!'

Carleton agreed with some feeling and, pressing her hands fleetingly, hurried off around the corner of the house.

Mr Foxcroft, who had overheard the proceedings through a crack in the library window, returned to his desk frowning pensively. He had to admit it, Carleton had surprised him. Indeed he had thought the night before that the young man was on the verge of delivering a sharp left to his jaw and had only been prevented by his presence in Mr Foxcroft's house as guest. To be sure, Carleton had seemed slightly nonplussed by his present situation, and Mr Foxcroft wondered just how he intended to possess himself of a carriage. He smiled slightly to himself and decided the young man deserved a helping hand. He thought for a minute or two and came to the conclusion that the venture was worth a small sacrifice. He rose, ensured that no crease marred the perfection of his biscuit-coloured pantaloons, and went in search of Miss Woodeforde.

Eliza's taste for needlework had always been minimal. Now, however, it afforded her considerable relaxation at a time when her brain was in something of a turmoil. Since Mr Foxcroft's departure she had been unsure of her feelings. Her continuance in Mr Foxcroft's house was irksome to her; she would greatly have preferred to have been gone before he returned, but this had proved impossible. She owed it to Sophy to remain, however little that damsel seemed to desire her presence. A click of the door made her raise her head, but the sight of Mr Foxcroft lounging against the jamb made her start and prick her finger. She gave an exclamation of distress and made a great show of sucking her finger to cover the embarrassment she felt.

Mr Foxcroft did not move. In fact he seemed rather to be enjoying her discomfort, for the suggestion of a smile was playing about the corner of his mouth. 'Why do you fuss so?' he asked her, his tone conversational. 'I am sure you have pricked your finger before and know you shall not die!'

'Of course I shall not!' she answered crossly. 'I am concerned merely for the fate of this handkerchief! I was embroidering it for your mother.' This was a lie and Mr Foxcroft seemed to sense it as such for he immediately came across the room to her side.

'Pray show me your work,' he said, smiling and holding out his hand. 'How kind it is to think of making my mother a present! I'm sure she will be quite delighted.'

He took the piece of cloth without waiting for permission and raised one brow. 'Miss Woodeforde, I had no idea you were such a fine needlewoman!'

She glanced fleetingly up at him. 'I dare say, sir, that there is a great deal about me you do not know!'

'Naturally so, since it has never pleased you to communicate the truth.'

She flushed and bit her lip. 'On one occasion only, sir, and that was your own fault!'

The brow lifted again and he stood above her, twisting the fine linen back and forth irritatingly. 'Are we to fight again? Come now, ma'am, I had thought the last time to be sufficient!'

She was scarlet now and looked up at him angrily. 'It is unkind in you to bring up such a thing! You must know I was—distressed.' She hesitated a moment and then said with an effort: 'I suppose I can no longer object to your marriage. If . . . you truly love Sophy then perhaps you may make her happy.'

He was startled and let the linen fall from his grasp. Muttering 'forgive me' he caught it up and dropped it in her lap. For a moment he was nonplussed, for he had counted upon her continued anger and disapproval. Then his lip curled. 'Indeed, Miss Woodeforde, that is monstrous kind in you! I only wish I could think I needed your approval!'

'Why you—'

This was better. Her eyes had flashed at him furiously and she had risen hastily from her chair, her embroidery slipping unheeded to the floor. 'Why will you not release my Sophy?' she demanded of him hotly. 'Can't you see how unhappy she is? Do you want to make her miserable for the rest of her life?'

He smiled infuriatingly. 'My dear Miss Woodeforde, I thought you had just decided I might make her happy after all!'

'No! Yes. Oh, you are positively—'

'Odious? Detestable?' Mr Foxcroft suggested helpfully since she appeared lost for words.

'Yes! And more, if I could only think of the right word to describe you!'

'How about hedgebird? Or loose fish, or something of that sort?' Miss Woodeforde fell silent and contemplated him smoulderingly, her breast rising and falling with some rapidity. The colour was high in her cheeks and one strand of hair had become detached from the rest and now lay across her face. Mr Foxcroft smiled and moved towards her. With one finger he lifted aside the offending lock of hair. 'You should not get so angry with me, you know,' he told her gently. 'I am really not so very wicked! Oh, I admit, I've had a mistress or two and I dare say I've treated them all quite shamefully, but I really have tired of it all! I don't want that sort of life any more and neither do I want a wife who will smile when I smile, tremble when I frown, and say yes to everything I can possibly suggest.'

Eliza did not move. He was very close to her now and was staring down at her with an expression that did curious things to her pulse-rate. For a moment she thought he would kiss her, and almost held her breath, but of a sudden he laughed and turned away.

'I shall not tell my mother your little secret,' he said lightly from near the door. 'Only I should pick it up, if I were you, or it will be quite horribly dirty before it is even finished.'

She stared blankly at him for a moment and then glanced where he pointed. As she bent to pick it up she heard the door open and when she raised her head he was gone.

CHAPTER TEN

Sophia slept very badly. She lay awake for several hours tossing and turning and when, finally exhausted, she was overcome by sleep she was tormented by Miss Woodeforde's reproaches and Mr Foxcroft pursuing her relentlessly in his curricle. When she awoke she felt drugged and heavy-eyed and her guilt weighed as heavily in the cold light of a grey, dismal day as it had done in the blackness of the night. She rose and dressed herself, forestalling the girl who came in with a mug of chocolate to help her with such tasks. She knew she could take nothing with her, but she regretted very little, except perhaps her first ball dress, which she suspected she would never see again. Realizing she might feel hungry later, she forced herself to swallow the chocolate, but the thought of breakfast made her feel sick. Consequently she dismissed the hovering girl absently and then pulled from the closet her new, warm pelisse. It felt heavy and hot, but she knew she might well need it before her adventure was concluded. The last thing she did before she left was to scribble a note to Miss Woodeforde. The writing was abominable and almost unreadable, but her haste was now so great that she barely noticed it, propping the note against the silver brushes on the dressing-table.

It was shortly after nine o'clock by this time and no reason existed that Miss Crawley should not take herself for a walk before breakfast. Her manner, however, was calculated to strike the most unsuspecting heart as odd, for she crept down the passage on tip-toe, straining her ears for the slightest sound. Indeed the noise of some distant door's banging with slightly too much force startled her so much that she dropped her reticule, spilling onto the carpet those items she had considered indispensible. Then, her hands shaking so much she could hardly control them, she finally managed to push her possessions away again and continued upon her treacherous journey to the hall.

With a lightness of heart in direct contrast to Miss Crawley's sober temper, Mr Foxcroft rose from his couch betimes, pulling the bell-rope imperiously for his valet. This worthy, startled from the homely but invaluable task of polishing his master's boots, was forced to scramble himself into his coat and, tucking the boots under one arm, scurried out of the servants' hall and up the cold stone backstairs, buffing the boots as he went. When he arrived in his master's chamber he was breathing a little faster than normal, but his demeanour was quite unruffled and he presented his master's boots as though they had been ready the night before.

'Jameson!' Mr Foxcroft exclaimed over his shoulder. 'Send Mr Davenham to me, there's a good fellow. And don't let him fob you off, it's a matter of some importance.'

'Mr Davenham, sir?' Jameson queried, reverentially standing the boots by the wall. 'If you will forgive me, sir, Mr Davenham is rarely abroad before noon.'

'A deplorable habit of which I am quite aware, Jameson. However, I do believe, if you present yourself in his chamber, you will find him probably already dressed, though perhaps a trifle short of temper.'

Jameson bowed. His conviction that Mr Davenham would be discovered in a darkened, silent chamber was so large that when his knock produced an impatient 'Come in, damn you!' he almost wished he had provided himself with a candle.

The room, however, was flooded with light. As his master had predicted, Mr Davenham was arisen and, at that moment, struggling with the recalcitrance of his boot. 'Damn it all, Collins!' he exclaimed without turning round, 'where the deuce have you been all this time? I'm sure if I had thought I should have to pull on my own boots I should have had myself engaged as a valet!'

Jameson coughed.

'For the Lord's sake, man, what are you waiting for? I warn you, there'll be the devil to pay if you don't move a leg!'

Jameson coughed again. 'May I be permitted to assist you, sir?'

Mr Davenham swore roundly. 'What's the matter with you, Collins? I warn you, this Turkish treatment will cut no wheedles with me!'

Jameson sighed and without more ado went to the gentleman's aid. When the boot was finally pulled up to Mr Davenham's satisfaction the young man stood up and contemplated himself in the glass. He did not seem much pleased with what he saw, but turning round to admonish his servant again he seemed struck by some salient point.

'You ain't Collins!'

'No, sir.'

'Then who the devil are you? Where's that Friday-faced fellow of mine?'

'I really have no conception, sir. I am the master's man, Jameson.'

'Well, you'll do, I suppose, though I shall take Collins to task when I see him, and so you may inform him too.'

'Begging your pardon, sir, but the master was anxious to see you at once in his chamber. It was that that brought me to you, sir.'

Mr Davenham stared. The rosy hue brought about by his exertions with the boot faded rapidly, to be replaced by an unearthly pallor. 'See me?' he repeated hoarsely. 'Now?'

'If you would, sir. He said it was a matter of some urgency.'

The gentleman eyed the valet wildly. 'Can't come, I'm afraid,' he managed in a croaking tone. 'Too devilish busy.'

'Begging pardon, sir, but the master instructed me not to permit myself to be—er—fobbed off.'

Mr Davenham rolled his eyes and wondered if he could plant the fellow a facer. He decided against it, however, and, strolling across the room, gathered a coat from a chair. 'Tell Mr Foxcroft I shall be with him directly,' he said, desperately hoping the terror he felt did not manifest itself in his voice.

'Very good, sir,' responded the valet, bowing and keeping his inevitable reflections to himself.

Carleton turned once more to the glass, apparently absorbing himself in the wonders of his cravat, but as soon as the door clicked shut he ran one despairing hand through his golden curls and stared wildly about the room, as if the answer to his problem were written upon its walls. After a moment or two, however, he seemed resolved, for he caught up his gloves and beaver and ran from the room. The passage was empty and he hurried past Mr Foxcroft's chamber without hindrance, but the hall below presented him with different problems. At the sight of Sterne, the butler, his eyes started wildly, but happily he recollected in time that he was not, as yet, quite a criminal. Accordingly he descended the stairs as slowly as his panic would allow, nodding carelessly to Sterne, and then, his boots clicking impatiently on the marble, hurried in the direction of the stables. He dared not think what he would do when he arrived; certainly the spectacle of a curricle and pair with an attendant groom did not figure among his wildest dreams. For a moment he hesitated in the doorway and then, as the groom touched his forelock, he strode forward, his step purposeful.

'I shall have to take the curricle!' he announced, trying to ignore the desperate pounding in his chest.

'Yessir,' said the groom, standing back. 'Mr Foxcroft said—'

'I'm sorry, I still have to take it!' So saying, he swung himself onto the high seat as the horses plunged away across the cobbles. The curricle swung and rattled out of the yard; for a moment Carleton thought it would turn over, then it steadied and bowled off at a fair pace down the drive. He knew now that he had committed the cardinal sin and that no forgiveness could ever be his. Mr Foxcroft's chestnuts were his pride; for Carleton to have stolen them was a dreadful, dreadful thing. With an effort he pushed these unwelcome thoughts from his brain. The horses were moving fast and he could see the lodge-gates in the distance. For a moment he thought he would be unable to stop their flight, but finally his heaving on the reins produced some slackening of speed and Carleton could only hope he had not ruined their mouths forever. The lodge-gates were before him now, but there was no sign of Sophia. He realized that he was probably earlier than he intended and was just wondering how long it would be before Mr Foxcroft came in pursuit when a small figure appeared from among the bushes.

Even before the horses drew up Carleton could see she was nervous. His own fears were nothing to the terror Sophia had felt whilst running through the Park and something of this communicated itself to him as he dragged her up beside him.

'Carleton!' she cried, dismayed. 'An *open* carriage?'

'Yes,' he answered grimly. 'I had no choice!'

'But dearest, it looks so . . . p-particular!'

So far from being in hot pursuit, Mr Foxcroft was relishing the unexpected but utterly successful turn his little plan had taken. Just how to provide the young man with a carriage had strained even Mr Foxcroft's intelligence and it had been his fear that Carleton, dolt though he undoubtedly was, would think his uncle's request, that he should convey the carriage to a friend in Maidenhead, just a trifle suspect. When Carleton had not, after all, appeared in his chamber he had stationed his valet by the window and that worthy's announcement, a few minutes later, that his master's curricle *and* valuable pair was being driven at breakneck speed down the avenue had produced an appreciative chuckle.

'It is to be hoped, sir, that Mr Davenham does not suffer An Accident!' Jameson said in slightly reproving tones.

'Unfortunately, I have no fear of it,' Mr Foxcroft returned, deplorably heartlessly, Jameson thought. 'Before long any attempt of his to drive like a lunatic will be greeted by screams of terror.'

Whether Jameson understood this cryptic remark or not Mr Foxcroft did not delay to discover. Satisfied with the arrangement of his cravat and the smooth perfection of his olive pantaloons, he strode from his chamber in his shirt-sleeves and disappeared down the passage that led to the west wing. If Jameson had thought to follow his master he would have been amazed indeed, for the gentleman walked without hesitation to Miss Crawley's door and without even the semblance of knocking entered the room. A few seconds later he reappeared, apparently pushing something into the pocket of his waistcoat, and the smile that twitched his mouth suggested he felt particularly pleased with the venture. Indeed when he sauntered into his room a few moments later the smile was still evident and did not disappear even as he absently permitted Jameson to assist him into his coat. Then, apparently quite unconcerned by the theft of his curricle, he wandered out of his chamber and down the stairs to the breakfast-room.

He was still seated there when, almost an hour later, Miss Eliza Woodeforde, her face heavy-eyed and drawn, entered the room. He had pushed his chair back from the table and now relaxed with his legs stretched out before him and indeed his legs were all Eliza could see since the upper part of his body was quite hidden by the *Morning Post*. There was no doubt in her mind as to who was behind that spread newspaper, for Eliza knew his hands, with their long fingers and square-cut emerald, quite as well as his face. She had slept remarkably ill. For some reason she had found herself much disturbed and the sight of Mr Foxcroft, abstracted though he patently was, was not a welcome one. At first she was glad that he took no notice of her, for she was female after all and felt she looked a perfect fright; but after a while a sensation of pique involuntarily made itself felt and she began to wonder if he were deliberately ignoring her. The small exclamations of amazement or dismay that periodically accompanied his reading served only to irritate her more, until she felt a quite shameful urge to rip the wretched newspaper into shreds. It was perhaps this violent inclination that finally communicated itself to Mr Foxcroft, for he suddenly closed his newspaper and laid it on the table.

197

'Good-morning, Miss Woodeforde!' he exclaimed, feigning surprise. 'Have you been here long?'

Miss Woodeforde glowered at him. She had, she knew, been making far more noise than was strictly lady-like during her breakfast, dropping her knife carelessly onto her plate and banging the various condiments about the table. 'Good-morning, Mr Foxcroft!' Eliza responded with a smile she hoped was as sickly as his own. 'Barely a minute, I assure you! You were so engrossed I did not care to disturb you.'

'Most thoughtful! But have you rung for coffee? This will be quite disgustingly cold, you know. I trust you have not been drinking it!'

'No, no, I have not.' Her eyes followed him with an expression of wrath as he crossed the room to the bell-rope. She hoped he would now leave her in peace, but to her annoyance he seemed determined to irritate her with his continued presence. Smiling, she thought, in a particularly inane manner, he had seated himself opposite her again and seemed inclined for conversation. Since her head was thumping quite unpleasantly by this time, she decided he was doing it purposefully to annoy her and consequently returned his bland inquiries after her health with replies bordering on the rude.

'I have been thinking,' Mr Foxcroft

remarked idly, 'that you seemed to be without your usual bloom, but perhaps I am tactless!'

'No more so, sir, I assure you, than I have come to expect.'

'Ah no, I suppose not.' Mr Foxcroft smiled irritatingly at her again. 'I had forgot. Your opinion of me was never very high, was it?'

'Since you have been at some pains to convince me of your badness that is not surprising, is it?'

He opened his eyes wide at her. 'I? My dear Miss Woodeforde, how can you say such things to me when I have been so hard pressed to make you think me not such a bad fellow!' He smiled. 'In fact I think, Miss Woodeforde, that you are finding it difficult not to like me very much indeed.'

Miss Woodeforde's fulminating reply was cut short by the entrance of the servant and until he had left them again she was obliged to hold her peace. Time, however, did nothing to temper her wrath. As soon as the door clicked shut she raised smouldering grey eyes to his smiling, placid countenance and said in a voice trembling with—violent—emotion: '*Like* you? Mr Foxcroft, I detest you! You are the most troublesome, irritating, proud, odious— *hedgebird* I have ever met in my life! And besides which,' she ended inconsequently, 'you're engaged to Miss Crawley.'

'So I am,' he concurred amiably. 'I shall not be, however, for very much longer.'

'You won't? What do you mean?'

He shrugged his shoulders and smiled infuriatingly. 'I have a feeling Miss Crawley will be marrying someone else.'

'Someone else?' Bewildered, Eliza laughed. 'Who else is there? She knows no one else!'

Mr Foxcroft continued to smile. 'As you say.' And with this he seemed to consider their conversation ended, for he rose, arriving at the door just as the servant entered with the coffee.

With Mr Foxcroft gone, Eliza was obliged to finish her repast in silent indignation. Since there was no one on whom she could vent her spleen she attacked her breakfast with some violence, drinking her coffee while it was still scalding hot and burning her throat. Rising, she went upstairs to fetch her wrap, intending to go for a brisk walk in the grounds to wear out her frustrations. Passing Sophia's chamber she knocked gently and peered round the door, but the room was empty and the bed already made. There was nothing unusual in this, for indeed Sophia had for some time been in the habit of rising betimes and wandering listlessly about the house and grounds. Consequently she thought little of it, experiencing merely a sense of irritation when she found Lady Ludlow standing watching her from her own doorway opposite.

'Miss Woodeforde!' this lady exclaimed, forcing a smile to her thin lips. 'I wish a word

·with you.'

'Very well, Lady Ludlow, I shall wait upon you later.'

'Now, young woman, if you please.'

'Very well.' If Lady Ludlow chose to entertain people when she looked such a fright it was none of Eliza's business. For the dowager had clearly been engaged in administering to her face and neck some complicated beauty treatment and it was with an elaborate negligée and lace cap that she had chosen to present herself in the passageway. Traces of some yellowish ointment were clearly visible about Lady Ludlow's nose and hair-line, and her whole face shone with all the luminosity of an oil-lamp. Without a word, however, Eliza followed her into her chamber, shutting the door and standing with her back to it.

'Come in, girl, for the Lord's sake!' Lady Ludlow exclaimed, glancing up irritably from the resumption of her smoothings and pattings. 'I cannot bear anyone hovering about me. That stupid Wellow is bad enough. I can't bear her by me, though she has a way with hair I've yet to see equalled.'

Eliza said nothing, but moved to where a small chair covered in faded chintz stood against the wall.

'Personally,' Lady Ludlow continued, staring disconsolately at her reflection, 'I'm not convinced at all by this new recipe. Sally

Darwin gave it to me saying it was quite marvellous for wrinkles and I must admit she did look—However, that's neither here nor there.' She turned her hard blue eyes upon Eliza and said: 'What think you about Mr Davenham, young woman?'

'Mr Davenham?' Eliza could recollect no very definite thoughts about the gentleman at all, but she said mildly: 'He is a very gentlemanlike young man, I am sure.'

'*Gentlemanlike?*' Lady Ludlow echoed, plainly disappointed. 'Of course he is gentlemanlike! He is the son of a peer! I mean, what think you of his person?'

'His person!' For a moment Carleton's gentle features eluded her and when they finally swam into her recollection she said with a slight smile: 'He is certainly very well, I'm sure no one can deny it.'

'Of course not,' Lady Ludlow concurred, somewhat appeased. 'As far as appearance is concerned I believe he could not be bettered.'

She stared hard at Eliza but she returned no answer, for indeed none readily occurred to her.

Lady Ludlow snorted to herself and returned to the contemplation of her face. 'Carleton is a man of great gentleness,' she continued. 'I have long observed it. In fact it was this that first made me take him up. At first I thought he and Mary—but she is too quick for him, I fear, for it must be owned he is sadly bird-witted. However, I have determined to do something for the fellow, and since our arrival at Ingham the answer has seemed plain.'

Eliza was mystified, wondering what form the assistance was to take. 'Madam, I fear I fail to understand exactly—'

Lady Ludlow suppressed her indignation with difficulty. 'It is plain, my good young woman, that you have never considered the problems a boy such as Carleton might face when it comes to matrimony. The gentlest of creatures, a perfect darling, I know, but sadly susceptible to the smooth-tongued! Only consider how easily he would be taken in!'

Eliza almost laughed. 'Truly, my lady, he is a catch for anybody, I am sure.'

'Naturally so,' Lady Ludlow concurred, nodding. 'I was persuaded we must see the thing in the same light.'

'Lady Ludlow, what "thing"? I'm afraid I don't—'

Lady Ludlow laughed shallowly. 'How droll you are, to be sure! But you need not think to pull the wool over my eyes, young woman! I have seen quite plainly where your ambitions lie and I may as well tell you, you have had my support from the beginning. It was never a match I approved of for—personal reasons.'

Eliza stared at her. 'Madam, what match? What are you talking of?'

'Lord, girl, are you trying to bamboozle me?

For if you are I tell you to your head it won't fadge. I'll have the thing without roundaboutation, if you please.'

Eliza drew herself up a little in her chair. 'Very well, my lady, I will speak plainly. Evidently the match you speak of is that between your brother and my charge. But what, pray, has Mr Davenham to say to anything?'

'Are you telling me, young woman,' Lady Ludlow said, her small eyes snapping beneath their puffy lids, 'that you have not been trying to throw Miss Crawley and my nephew together?'

'Sophia and *Carleton?*' For a moment Eliza stared and then she started to laugh. 'That is perfectly ridiculous!'

'Ridiculous or not, they have been making calves' eyes at each other for this past week or more and if you did not see it you've a great deal more hair than wit!' Lady Ludlow concluded inelegantly.

'*Making calves' eyes?*' Eliza repeated frowning. 'You mean, Mr Davenham has been making approaches to Miss Crawley?'

The older woman laughed harshly. 'Oh yes, and she has shown no distaste for them, I can assure you! Why, I dare say they're together at this moment, if you only knew it!'

'But this is appalling!' Eliza exclaimed, rising in some haste. 'If you had seen it I wish you had apprised me of it!'

'Miss Woodeforde, the matter was plain to anyone. All I can say is, you must have been mightily wrapped up in your own affairs if it passed you by, that's all!'

'I must find Mr Foxcroft,' Eliza cried, scarcely heeding her. 'If this is true there is no time to be lost!'

'I doubt,' the dowager said, smiling thinly, 'whether you will find him a very sympathetic listener.' But she spoke to thin air. Miss Woodeforde, leaving the room in some haste, hurried away without even closing the door.

When he had left her Mr Foxcroft had gone straight to his mother's bed-chamber. He knew she would not care to see him quite so early but that could not be avoided; there was something he had to tell her and he would not have much more time in which to do it. As he had expected, she refused admittance, sending Millie with a message that he was not to present himself again before midday. Mr Foxcroft had paid little attention to it. Being assured that Mrs Foxcroft was sitting up in bed reading her mail, he had put Millie gently but firmly to one side and marched into the room. Cutting short his fond parent's scathing remarks about his manners and want of propriety, he had planted a kiss on the withered surface of her cheek and told her his news. Mrs Foxcroft's relief that, somehow or other, her daughter's scheming had had the desired results was but fleeting. The information that her son's engagement was, perforce, at an end was followed by the devastating intelligence that he was apparently about to contract an alliance even more inappropriate and one not even sanctioned by the promise of wealth.

'Julius, the female is little more than a governess!'

'Yes, darling, I know, but a governess with a lineage as proud and as lengthy as our own.'

Mrs Foxcroft eyed him doubtfully.

'Her uncle is an Earl,' Mr Foxcroft reminded her gently.

'Yes,' the good woman responded, 'but her father was cut off without a sou and sent packing to India and that can't have been for no reason.'

'I believe her father to have been something of a romantic, Mother,' Julius Foxcroft pronounced, his dark eyes twinkling. 'And surely you cannot blame his daughter for his folly?'

'Of course I can!' Mrs Foxcroft told him roundly. 'Lord, Julius, I begin to think you have a screw loose!'

Mr Foxcroft laughed. 'Perhaps I have, I can't tell! I only know my life will be damnable without her and that should be enough for you, I know it is for me.'

Mrs Foxcroft sighed. 'If you really mean that, Julius—but good gracious, boy, why does this all have to be done in such a slapdash manner? Whatever will people think?'

A wicked gleam showed in Mr Foxcroft's expressive eye. 'I care that for the world,' he answered, snapping his fingers, 'and so does she. Besides, what use have I for all the trappings and frills of a society affair? This is far, far better.' He grinned suddenly. 'And anyway,' he said, patting one thin hand, 'I believe I'm something of a romantic myself.'

*   *   *

Eliza had begun to panic. Her rapid search of the house had failed to produce not only Mr Foxcroft, but Sophia and Carleton as well. Questioning servants at random, she had finally elicited the information that Sophia had gone out alone for a walk, but nothing had been seen of Mr Davenham. She had run outside and into those walks Sophia most frequently chose, but without success, and it was as she hurried back towards the house that she encountered Mr Foxcroft. He was striding towards her, his face unnaturally grim.

'Oh sir!' she exclaimed, barely noticing his expression or the paper he held, 'I have been looking for you! Have you seen Sophia? Miss Crawley?' She stared up at him anxiously and only now did she begin to observe the severity of his countenance.

'Miss Woodeforde, I have been looking for you.' He held out the piece of paper and Eliza, her hand shaking so much she could hardly control it, finally managed to snatch it from his grasp. At first she read it so fast she did not understand a word. Then, forcing herself to be calm, she took control of her nerves and read:

'Dear Eliza,
'Forgive me! There was nothing else I could do! I shall love no one else but Carleton and cannot marry Mr Foxcroft *ever*.' This word was underlined several times. 'I know what I am doing to be wicked, but I pray that you, Eliza, may understand and forgive me.
'Your loving friend,
'Sophy.'

The note was scrawled and several words had been lined through. In places the ink had run as though she had been crying.

'Good God,' Eliza said hollowly. 'She is not *dead*?'

Mr Foxcroft shook his head and the vice-like grip on Eliza's heart slackened a little. 'I believe them to have eloped, Miss Woodeforde. My curricle and pair are missing from the stables.'

'Your *curricle*?' Eliza echoed, horrified. 'An *open* carriage?'

The gentleman nodded. 'I was preparing to go out myself. In his urgency Carleton possessed himself of the first equipage that came to hand.' He paused as if struck by some unpleasant thought. 'Good God,' he said hollowly, 'he may kill them!'

'*Kill* them?' Eliza whispered hoarsely. 'He cannot drive?'

'Devil a bit! And the beasts are the finest I could get.'

'The *beasts*? Who cares about the horses, Mr Foxcroft, when they may be in danger themselves?'

The gentleman stared. 'In danger themselves?' he repeated. 'What nonsense! An odd scratch or two, should they take a tumble, but one of my *chestnuts* could break a leg!'

Eliza stared at him with loathing. 'I must go after them,' she said with resolution. 'Will you summon me a carriage?'

'A carriage, Miss Woodeforde? Do you propose to go after them yourself alone?'

'Naturally, sir! Miss Crawley is in my charge!'

'And how, madam, do you propose to persuade them to come back? You could not knock out young Davenham.'

'Knock him out?' Eliza echoed, startled. 'Why should I need to do that, pray?'

Mr Foxcroft smiled. 'Carleton has no brain, Miss Woodeforde. Any remonstrations of yours will be useless, I can assure you. By now he will almost certainly have worked himself into a panic, convinced he could be hanged and drawn for what he has done.'

'But that's nonsense!' Eliza exclaimed,

almost laughing.

'Is it? What do you know of Carleton, Miss Woodeforde? What do you know of a mind so shallow that it can be overborne by the slightest suggestion? Believe me, by now Davenham will have convinced himself he is a desperate criminal.'

Eliza was silent. She knew what Mr Foxcroft meant, for Sophia was the same, quite likely to be overcome by the merest suggestion. 'I am amazed they ever thought of it!' she exclaimed, as the enormity of their nerve hit her.

'So am I,' Mr Foxcroft concurred solemnly. 'But I think someone might have put the idea into their minds.'

She looked up sharply, apparently struck, and seemed about to make some remark, but after a brief hesitation all she said was: 'Mr Foxcroft, I am resolved to go in pursuit. They will be obliged to stop to change horses and I may have news of them. But do you think—' She looked up at him again, her eyes pleading. 'Sir, would you escort me? If it is as you say, then perhaps between us we might persuade them to come home. After all, Miss Crawley is your fiancée.'

'Come with you, Miss Woodeforde? Indeed I don't know. I had planned—'

'Oh! How callous men are! How glad I am I never married! Can you not see how terrible this is for them? Do you want me to go on my knees to you?'

He contemplated her gravely. 'No, Miss Woodeforde, the sight is not one I should find edifying. However, if you are convinced that my presence is necessary I shall of course place myself at your disposal.'

Eliza drew herself up a little. 'Thank you,' she said stiffly. 'I shall fetch my reticule. I should be grateful if you did not disclose the— true reason for our outing.'

Mr Foxcroft bowed, his face grave. As soon as she had rounded the corner of the house, however, he started to chuckle and by the time he had reached the stables he was laughing.

CHAPTER ELEVEN

Mr Foxcroft's elegant travelling carriage rattled and shuddered on the uneven road. For a short distance out of Ingham the road had been in good repair, but all too soon had deteriorated into the pot-holed and rutted state that characterised the Berkshire roads. The wheels dropped mercilessly into the pockets made by weeks of bad weather, splashing the darkly muddy water against the windows, where it ran down in little trickles, and throwing the passengers against the sides of the carriage. For some time Eliza had sat in silence, staring unseeingly out of the smeared window, barely aware of the quiet figure beside her. He was very aware of her.

Watching her anxiously twisted fingers and bitten lip, he suffered a momentary pang of conscience and it was only his love of the absurd that enabled him to remain silent. Miss Woodeforde was plainly tormenting herself; that much was obvious. He decided that he must be a very hard-hearted man not to put her out of her misery. But as the coach rattled northwards, Mr Foxcroft sat smiling to himself in his corner.

By the time they had made the first change Eliza's head was thumping painfully. At the toll-gates Mr Foxcroft had descended into the fine drizzle to ask if the curricle had been seen and, had it not been quite necessary, Eliza would have been sorely tried to keep her temper. As it was, she had chewed her lip nearly raw at the waste of time involved, picturing every minute Sophy with a broken neck, lying in a ditch. She was only too aware also of the speed possible in a sporting carriage and of the anxiety of the young couple to press on with all haste. However, the change was effected with almost unnatural speed, she noticed in spite of her abstraction, and they were back on the road before that consuming impatience had taken hold of her once more.

'Tell me, was there any news?' She had turned large eyes towards him, the anxiety showing plainly.

'They are an hour ahead of us,' he answered

expressionlessly.

'An hour!' Eliza's heart sank. The reports at the toll-gates had placed the young couple barely forty-five minutes away. The news came as a bitter blow. 'Then they are drawing ahead.'

'It would seem,' Mr Foxcroft said, in a matter-of-fact tone, 'that Davenham is extremely anxious. The ostler was quite affronted by what I gather was Carleton's excessive urgency.'

'Then what hope have we, sir? It seems impossible.' Eliza's tone was dull and her head dropped against the side of the carriage.

'Unless Carleton is a fool they will be obliged to put up somewhere tonight. We may overtake them then.'

'Tonight!' Eliza stared at him. She realised now that she had unconsciously expected to have overtaken them well before nightfall. 'Mr Foxcroft, if they spend a night on the road—'

The gentleman did not answer.

'How could I be so stupid!' she exclaimed, wringing her hands in time-honoured fashion. 'If only I had not been so wrapped up in myself I would have seen it all! However shall I explain it to Sir Lucius?'

Mr Foxcroft smiled wryly. 'Is that your primary concern?'

'Of course not!' Some of the old fire had returned to her voice. 'But he will be very much distressed in any event when he hears of

213

this adventure.'

The gentleman appeared to give the matter consideration. 'You think he will not approve of Carleton?'

Eliza stared at him. 'That is not the question, sir! I'm sure the young man is quite well in his way, but an elopement! Surely you can see how disastrous it is?'

'Oh, indeed!' Mr Foxcroft agreed, grinning unaccountably. 'But I am relieved to hear you are not opposed to Davenham himself.'

'I hardly know him, Mr Foxcroft. However, doubtless he is well enough, and if Sophia had told me—'

'He will be a very wealthy man, Miss Woodeforde,' Mr Foxcroft said, interrupting her gravely. 'As far as eligibility is concerned he is a great deal more eligible than I! Not only is his fortune greater than mine and his lineage longer, but when his father dies he will be a peer and that, you should know, is enough to convince the most knaggy old parent around!'

'Then why did he behave in such a foolish way?'

Mr Foxcroft shrugged. 'You must have observed him, Miss Woodeforde; he is not a fellow of—outstanding mental ability. Almost certainly some unknown fear has lodged itself in his brain and he sees this as the only escape. It is merely unfortunate that Miss Crawley's intelligence is not sufficient to banish his misconceptions.'

For a moment the gentleman thought she would take up cudgels in defence of her darling, but after a second or two she said pensively, 'In that respect they are very well matched.'

Mr Foxcroft settled back without an answer, well satisfied with the progress they had made.

By the time they had reached Maidenhead Eliza's anxiety appeared somewhat allayed. To be sure, she was still eager to overtake them before nightfall, but the agitated wringing of the hands had ceased and a determined expression had replaced the worried frown. By three o'clock that afternoon the gnawing pangs of hunger persuaded her to succumb to Mr Foxcroft's entreaties and they lunched at Princes Risborough, but the meal was a scrambled affair and Eliza was now very silent. They were still nearly an hour behind Sophy and within two hours it would be dark. Mr Foxcroft also seemed withdrawn and when she glanced at him Eliza saw his brow furrowed in thought. Absently marking the forms of trees and bushes beneath the slaty sky, she reached a sudden decision, reluctant at first, but growing ever stronger as she considered it. She had no intention now of standing in Carleton's way. Convinced as she was that Sophia would never have agreed to such an undertaking were her heart not seriously engaged, she began to realize how much better for her than

Mr Foxcroft would Mr Davenham be. Glancing covertly at the gentleman, she wondered what he truly felt about the escapade, but her nerve failed at asking him. She had never considered his heart involved, but she decided suddenly that their departure must be a severe blow to his pride at least and realized that he was behaving with unaccustomed forbearance. He had settled back in his seat now and she saw, with some astonishment, that he intended to sleep. Wondering how in the world he could do such a thing, she closed her eyes likewise and in a moment had fallen fast asleep herself.

Mr Foxcroft watched her in some contentment. The light was failing rapidly, the darkness hastened by the heavy sky, and, peering at his watch, he saw it was nearing five o'clock. It was some little while now since he had inquired after the runaways at either toll-gate or change and an objective observer might have considered him curiously unconcerned. Peering through the window, he considered their position for some few minutes and then, as loudly as he dared, for fear of waking the lady, he tapped his cane upon the roof. After a moment there came a muffled response and the gentleman leaned back, an expression of some amusement on his face.

The motion of the chaise was rapid and uneven. Joggled as she was in her seat Eliza found herself able to sleep, but the gentle rolling down of the carriage, followed by standstill and silence, was enough to jerk her suddenly awake. She opened her eyes to unexpected darkness and the impression that the carriage was empty but for her. After a little while, however, she realized that the opposite door stood open and that her companion seemed to be conversing with his coachman. In a minute or two this impression was confirmed by the rectangle of doorway being obscured by the shape of a man's head.

'We've broken a trace,' Mr Foxcroft said clearly, 'and unfortunately Blackett has omitted to put a spare in the boot.' He climbed back into the carriage now and sat down with a sigh. 'It's a devil of a nuisance, but Blackett has taken one of the horses to the next town.'

Eliza forced her numbed brain to accept these new facts. 'How far is that?' she asked presently.

She could just see his shrug. 'Who knows? To be honest I have not much idea where we are—I've been asleep.'

'But—he could be hours! How can we just sit here?'

In the darkness Mr Foxcroft smiled. 'There is very little else we can do, Miss Woodeforde, unless you care to mount a carriage horse yourself.'

Since this was clearly not a serious suggestion Eliza ignored it. She was staggered at his apparent unconcern and said with barely suppressed emotion, 'You realize, sir, that we have now little hope of overtaking Miss Crawley?'

For a moment he did not answer and Eliza felt she could almost have hit him in her impatience. 'I do realize it, Miss Woodeforde,' he answered, quite calmly.

Eliza breathed deeply. 'I am relieved,' she said dryly, 'that you take the situation so philosophically. Miss Crawley being my responsibility, however, I find it rather more difficult to be complacent!'

Mr Foxcroft was making small movements in the dark that suggested that he was straightening his cuffs. 'I'm afraid, Miss Woodeforde, that we have never, from the moment we headed north, had the remotest chance of overtaking the young couple.'

Eliza stared at where she knew him to be. There was something almost apologetic in his tone and she did not trust it. 'What do you mean?'

The gentleman sighed. 'I mean that they are not, and never have been, heading for Scotland.'

'Are not—But how can this be? Have we not had continual reports of their progress?'

He shook his head, the movement outlined against the dimness that was the window. 'I made the reports to you, certainly, but I have to admit that they were entirely fabricated.'

Eliza did not answer at once. There was

218

more to this than she yet knew and she was trying hard not to let her temper be her master. 'What about Miss Crawley's note? It was her writing!'

'Of course. The note was genuine. I dare say that by this time Davenham and Miss Crawley are at Malham Park.'

'Malham?' Nothing, Eliza felt, could have been less in her expectations. 'But why?'

In the darkness he smiled at her. 'Carleton is an old-fashioned fellow, my dear. He is also a mountain of propriety. Where else should he go?'

'But this is ridiculous! What can he possibly hope to achieve?'

'Everything, I should imagine,' Mr Foxcroft responded coolly. 'I had rather thought it the time-honoured practice to request the hand of a lady from her father.'

Eliza forced a laugh. 'You understand Sir Lucius less than I gave you credit for, sir! Have you forgotten already how anxious he was to see Sophy married to you?'

'Indeed not,' the gentleman responded with some feeling. 'In fact it has been the devil's own task for me to find a way out of the dashed affair!' He sensed her amazement and laughed. 'Oh, yes! On the one hand there was Crawley threatening me with the law, should I dare to recant; and on the other my family and yourself with pressure of every other kind to persuade me to do just that! I was in the devil's own fix, as you may well see!' He paused, apparently in contemplation of his late predicament. 'However, a solution finally presented itself, though I must admit I needed some assistance.' He grinned at her in the dark. 'It was Carleton himself, you see. Like the rest of us—except perhaps yourself—I had seen quite plainly what a cake of himself Carleton was making and yet it was beyond me how to turn it to my advantage, especially since that little fool Sophia seemed determined to turn him down.' Mr Foxcroft ignored Eliza's indignant interpolation. 'It was only when I was in London that the solution came to me in a flash, as it were, but I needed to arouse Carleton's wrath, as well as plant the idea into his sodden brain. But fortunately the poor fellow is quite as much of a slow-top as everybody thinks him and it only needed the odd drunken suggestion of how I might comport myself after my marriage to bring to the fore all his chivalrous emotions. That, together with the suggestion that he should always approach a girl's father first when he wished to become leg-shackled, was all he needed to send him to Miss Crawley's rescue.' He smiled. 'And there you have it. By this time they will be in Bath and no doubt enjoying all the warmth of the old buffer's favour.'

Although stunned by this incredible monologue, Eliza made herself speak. 'This is absolutely ridiculous,' she advanced, forcing her temper under control. 'Quite apart from the sheer nerve of what you have done, Sir Lucius will never accept such a thing! I don't know how you could imagine it for a moment!'

She had an infuriating idea that Mr Foxcroft was for some reason enjoying her rage. 'Simple, my dear ma'am! Before leaving London I communicated the whole matter to him by express. This very morning I had an answer—somewhat terse, it is to be admitted—but saying that if I wished to dispatch the young man to Malham he would be very pleased to receive him.' He pondered a moment. 'No doubt his daughter's somewhat hysterical return might perplex him, but doubtless they will sort it out between themselves.'

He had left her without a thing to say. So completely had he arranged matters that even through her infuriation she had to admire him and it was some moments before she realized that she was still sitting abandoned somewhere on the Scotland road. A succession of unwelcome ideas followed rapidly on this realization, but instead of panic she experienced a sense of deprivation and a foolhardy inclination to burst into tears. She swallowed hard, however, recollected that there was a pistol in the holster at her elbow and said as boldly as she could, 'If they are now in Bath, Mr Foxcroft, what are we doing here?'

221

She sensed him grinning again. 'I have abducted you,' he answered solemnly.

'Ab—ducted me?' Miss Woodeforde heard her voice give a peculiar squeak, and giggled, to her amazement.

'Indeed.' Mr Foxcroft's tone was sepulchrally grave. 'You see, ma'am, in London I reached a decision. It came to me as—' here he gestured dramatically at the open doorway— 'a blow from above!'

There was something so ridiculous in his manner that Eliza truly felt inclined to laugh. 'What did?'

'That I could not live without you,' he answered simply, abandoning abruptly his ridiculous attitude of a moment before. Eliza not answering, he continued: 'You had made it so very plain, you see, how perfectly repulsive you have found me that I decided to emulate one of my ancestors, Frederick Foxcroft. You told me once that I had a look of him, do you recall? His reputation was somewhat unsavoury, I believe, and he was considered rather a Bluebeard. Imprisoning damsels in the dungeons was very much to his taste.'

'The dungeons?' The whole thing was now so ridiculous that Eliza could not help laughing. 'Where? At Ingham?'

'Undoubtedly not! In Colgray Castle, not very far from this spot.'

'Colgray—? I've never heard of it!'

'We're on our way there now, or at least we

were, until that fool Blackett abandoned us.'

'Really, Mr Foxcroft, this is too fanciful for words! Do you really intend to *imprison* me?'

He shook his head. 'Of course not! I'm not so barbaric, I hope, that I resort to such measures. No, I shall merely keep you out all night until you are so hopelessly compromised that you have no recourse but to marry me.'

'Mr Foxcroft, nothing in the world would persuade me to marry you!'

'It won't?' For a moment the gentleman sounded truly discouraged. 'Then you really find me quite repugnant?'

Eliza hesitated. There was that in his voice that confused her. 'You are taking an unfair advantage, sir,' she told him earnestly. 'How can you possibly hope to persuade me in circumstances like these?'

'Could I have persuaded you in any other way?'

'Yes—No!—Oh, how can I tell? The whole thing is too ridiculous for words!'

'It is?'

'Of course! Until five minutes ago I thought you were engaged to Miss Crawley!'

'But if I hadn't been how would you have felt? Tell me!'

He had drawn considerably nearer to her on the seat and she could feel the nearness of his body. He seemed to be breathing very quickly and her own pulses started racing in response. 'I . . . I don't know, sir! It is so . . . unexpected!'

'What flummery!' he told her roundly. 'You've known it since the first time we met and so have I! For you to deny it is to deny your own heart and you know it. Look at me.'

She did so, even though she could barely see the outline of his head.

'Admit it! You've known it and so have I!'

He had her hand now and was gripping it firmly, the grip of a strong, determined man. She did know it, she did admit it and she nodded slowly.

'Then you will marry me.' It was a statement, not a question.

'No! I don't know! How can I? I have so little! Only think how angry your mother and sister will be!'

'Mother knows already and, as for Antonia, I don't care a rush what she thinks.'

Eliza was stunned. It was all too fast, too hurried for her to comprehend, and even if she agreed it would seem he still intended to compromise her name. 'Even if I said yes, what then? We are still out in the middle of nowhere, with no coachman and no prospect of getting anywhere!'

'Eliza, if at this moment I could, by some miracle, transport us to a perfectly respectable house where no one could possibly raise their brows at either of us, would you marry me then?'

She hesitated, more for effect than thought, for she was not lacking in sense of drama herself. Besides, he deserved to suffer a little. Finally she said softly, 'I would.'

Mr Foxcroft released her hand and leant back against the squabs with a deep sigh. She realized suddenly how taut his whole body had been, how tense his voice and manner. After a moment he reached out and pulled shut the door. Banging on the roof with his cane, he said shortly, 'Very well, Blackett, you may drive on.'

The carriage rolled gently away. Eliza could hear the clopping of the horses and the indistinct cries of the coachman above them. As the realization of what he had done swept over her, she turned to Mr Foxcroft, only wishing he could see how very angry she was. 'How *dare* you!' she managed in a voice trembling with the violence of her feelings. 'How could you trick me in such an— *ungentlemanly* way?'

The gentleman did not seem too perturbed. 'Eliza, my dear girl, what a very great goose you are! Can you not see what I have done? How long, in the situation at Ingham, could you have held out against me? Forever, I should imagine, even had I managed to convince you that Carleton and Sophia were meant for each other. Noble sentiments about your worth and position, or some such foolishness, would undoubtedly have sent you in search of some new position and then what hope would there have been for me, since you would probably do your utmost to get yourself lost?' He reached out and took her hand again. 'You know I love you. You know too what my life would be like without you, don't you? What have I done that is so very wrong? Tell me, my love!'

She could not answer. Her heart was too full; besides, she did not feel able to acknowledge the truth of what he had said without bursting into tears.

He patted her hand reassuringly. 'Do you want a handkerchief, child? We are almost there, you see, and I want you to look your best.'

Eliza jerked up her head. The lights of a lodge were just passing by and dimly in the distance she could just distinguish the outline of some enormous building, illuminated in one or two downstairs windows.

'Where are we?' she asked, her voice a nervous whisper.

'Hush, my love, you will see in a moment.'

The carriage was rolling down a driveway that very evidently was in some need of repair, since the wheels fell frequently into its pits and potholes, and once she heard the coachman urging his beasts to 'Come up, there!' The house looming before them was certainly of vast size and probably great antiquity, since it rambled in a somewhat random manner about an enormous area of land and sported at one end two round towers darkly silhouetted

226

against the night sky.

'Where are we?' she asked him, her voice anxious. 'Is it Colgray?'

'It is indeed,' came the cheerful answer. 'Come, I will help you down.' The carriage had certainly stopped and Eliza had no choice but to obey, since Mr Foxcroft had thrown open the door himself and jumped down and now stood waiting for her to follow him. Bemused and not a little afraid, she allowed him to hand her down and then stood staring as a dark figure appeared in the enormous doorway, a lantern held dramatically overhead.

'So you are come at last! Good gracious, what extraordinary travelling hours you young persons have! Well, come along, come along. My dinner is already on the table, though I dare swear Miss Benjamin will be able to find something for you.'

Eliza stared in amazement at the figure in the outmoded black dress who had thus heralded them. Glancing up at Mr Foxcroft, she saw him smiling, but without that touch of malice and mischief that generally characterised him. She took his proffered arm and they entered the house.

'Good gracious!' exclaimed Miss Stanley again, assimilating Eliza's flimsy wrap. 'Whatever were you thinking of, child? Come away, away, do, from that dreadful door! The chimneys smoke enough as it is.' She led them into a very high-vaulted room, the recesses of which the single lantern she yet held could not hope to penetrate. 'I dare say you think this a dreadful old place, but it suits me and I suit it, so come along.' She led the way briskly across the hall and through an arched doorway and thence along a series of stony passages to a small spiral stairway. 'Mind your step, children, for the Lord's sake! This is where my father broke his neck.'

In silence they mounted the narrow stairway, arriving at last at an immensely thick doorway that stood open onto another passage. Their tread was somewhat softened now by an elderly carpet and from somewhere near at hand came the bark of a dog.

Jemima Stanley threw open a door. A room, unexpectedly cosy and small, was arranged as a living-room, furnished with old, comfortable chairs and heated by a blazing, cheering, log fire. Another door led to a further chamber and it was here in what had plainly once been the servants' quarters that Miss Stanley made her home.

'Come in, come in! Don't stand there gawping! I dare say you think I should be shut up in bedlam, but it suits me very well to live up here, with just old Benjy to keep me company. Bring some more food, Benjy; can't you see we have guests?' An old woman who had appeared at a farther doorway grunted and disappeared again and in a moment they found themselves served with steaming soup.

'I don't stand upon ceremony, as you see,' Miss Stanley announced, drawing out a chair. 'Sit down. I was expecting you as you see.'

They sat and ate. The atmosphere, while primitive, was warm and friendly and, while Jemima wasted no effort on the finer things of life, Eliza found herself more at ease and comforted than for years. The meal was simple but sufficient and finally Miss Stanley said: 'There's port, young man, if you want it. It's a fine drop, my father laid it down, but if you'll excuse me I have other business.' She strode to the door, but said over her shoulder: 'Besides, I dare say you've things to talk about.'

'This is really Colgray?' Eliza asked when she had left them alone.

He nodded. 'This is what your Sophy will inherit one day. I couldn't think of anywhere else to bring you and Jemima's as game as a pebble, you know. I had no trouble at all in persuading her.'

Eliza pondered. 'Then you intended this all the time?'

He smiled at her. 'Yes, darling. You didn't really think I would compromise you, did you?'

She did not answer and he laughed. 'Come, say you'll forgive me.'

'How long are we staying?'

'Until we're married. I thought you would want Jemima to give you away. I understand there's a delightful little church just over the hill.'

Eliza turned up at him, her grey eyes anxious. 'Julius, tell me! Are you really sure you want to marry me?'

'More than anything in the world.'

'But—'

'But what?'

Eliza shrugged and smiled and Mr Foxcroft, since he had nothing else to say, kissed her instead.

We hope you have enjoyed this Large Print book. Other Chivers Press or Thorndike Press Large Print books are available at your library or directly from the publishers.

For more information about current and forthcoming titles, please call or write, without obligation, to:

Chivers Press Limited
Windsor Bridge Road
Bath BA2 3AX
England
Tel. (01225) 335336

OR

Thorndike Press
295 Kennedy Memorial Drive
Waterville
Maine 04901
USA

All our Large Print titles are designed for easy reading, and all our books are made to last.